COLOR HIM GAY

Being the Further Adventures of

That Man from C.A.M.P.

I0638422

by

Victor J. Banis

The Borgo Press
An Imprint of Wildside Press

MMVII

♠ CONTENTS ♠
λ

♠ FOREWORD ♠
TO THE SECOND EDITION
λ

The books in the series, *The Man from C.A.M.P.*, were among the earliest of the many novels I have penned. They were written in the 1960s, and they are very much a part of that exciting era when people of so many different sorts were coming out of so many different closets. Gay people were celebrating in the streets the very same lifestyle that only a few years before had engendered in many of us guilt and shame and fear, ruined large numbers of promising careers and sent many to prison.

These books were a part of my celebration. They were written with tongue very firmly in cheek, in a few days each, with nary a thought of rewrite or polishing up some admittedly amateurish prose. They were never intended to be "literature," and they are not. They were, however, intended to be fun.

I think they still are.

—Victor J. Banis
July 2006

♠ THE MAN FROM C.A.M.P. ♠
CHECKLIST
λ

1. *The Man from C.A.M.P.*
2. **Color Him Gay*
3. *The Watercress File*
4. *The Son Goes Down*
5. *Gothic Gaye*
6. *Holiday Gay*
7. *Rally Round the Fag*
8. **The Gay Dogs*
9. *Blow the Man Down*
10. *Gay-Safe* (not written by Victor Banis)

*=Published by Wildside Press

Associated Titles:

Sex and the Single Gay
The C.A.M.P. Guide to Astrology
The C.A.M.P. Cookbook

♠ <u>Chapter One</u> ♠
λ

Jackie Holmes smiled over the rim of his glass at the good-looking young redhead in the mirror behind the bar. The redhead smiled back and continued to play kneesies with him.

Definitely encouraging, Jackie thought. He turned slightly on his seat while still maintaining the enjoyable pressure of their legs, and faced the stranger.

"All alone?" he asked to break the ice.

"I was. But I'd just as soon not be," the redhead said.

Jackie smiled again and studied his neighbor quickly but thoroughly. The redhead was not much taller than his own five feet, nine inches, but with a stockier build. While Jackie was slender and small of build, the young man opposite him displayed, in his jeans and a tight fitting T-shirt, a sculptured and muscular body. The enticing bulge of his jeans made the overall picture even more enticing. Brown eyes twinkled at Jackie from the freckled and young looking face.

"My name's Jackie" He extended his hand.

"I'm Bob," the redhead answered, shaking Jackie's hand firmly.

The evening, Jackie decided, was progressing nicely. He had been in two other bars before this one, all of them gay, and all of them rather quiet. In fact, he had all but decided to call it a night and return home when the sexy redhead had taken a seat beside him at the bar. Now he was not so eager to go home; at least, not by himself.

"Want another drink?" Jackie asked him with a meaningful gaze that managed to ask other questions.

"I don't really need it," Bob informed him. His eyes were doing a good job of answering Jackie's silent questions and the answers were all favorable.

"That's encouraging."

"I live just a couple of blocks from here," Bob explained. "Why don't you come up for some coffee or something?"

"I'll accept, on both counts," Jackie answered. "What's the address?"

The redhead gave him the address and Jackie committed it efficiently to memory. "I'll join you there in a couple of minutes," he said.

He watched as the redhead left the bar. The view from the back was just as interesting. His buttocks were lush spheres of flesh, neither too lean nor too fat, tightly encased in the jeans that did more to reveal the shape of things to come than to conceal.

Jackie downed the rest of his drink and, with an expectant tingle in his loins, left the bar a minute later.

The parking lot was in the rear. He circled around the building, entered the comparative darkness of the lot and approached his car. The sound of a scuffle from nearby brought him to a halt.

He paused for a second beside his car. There was a fight in progress, in the narrow space that separated the bar from the neighboring building. By all rights he should investigate and do what he could to straighten things out. On the other hand, there was a sexy young redhead just a few blocks away, waiting for him to arrive.

With a sigh Jackie moved past his car and started for the fight. Business, he reminded himself, before pleasure.

The fight was decidedly a one-sided affair. Of the four people involved, three of them were busily engaging in working over the fourth. For his part the victim was putting up a good fight, if a losing one. Tall and lanky, with what gave the appearance of a long blond fright wig atop his head, he was backed now to the wall, using hands and feet alike to fight off his attackers.

As Jackie paused at the beginning of the narrow passageway, there was a click of metal and the moonlight gleamed on the blade of a knife. It was time, Jackie decided, starting to run, that someone evened out the battle.

The man with the knife heard the sound of his approach and whirled about to face him. Jackie was faster, catching the shadowy figure in half turn. He grabbed for the knife hand, giving the wrist a violent yank that sent the man off balance. A knee to the groin finished the job. The knife fell to the ground as the man doubled in pain.

Someone grabbed Jackie from behind. With lightning speed Jackie fell forward, carrying his attacker up and over to send him flying through the air.

With only one combatant, the blond victim of the attack was faring better. Jackie came toward him, grabbing hold of the remaining antagonist, a burly six-foot figure. The man slipped from his grasp and landed a hard fist on Jackie's jaw. Staggering backward, Jackie caught the edge of a brick that, if it had landed squarely, would have probably caved in his scalp. As it was, he sank to his knees, dazed momentarily.

The trio of hoods, however, had had enough. They took advantage of the opportunity to break away, disappearing into the parking lot. By the time Jackie had gotten to his feet, a car had roared to life in the lot, and a second later it raced away with a squeal of tires.

He turned instead to the blond, who had been felled also by a parting blow. To his amazement, however, the blond was no longer a blond. The golden mane had been a wig after all and it had been lost in the scuffle.

"Girl, you sure pick them tough," Jackie said, helping the stranger to his feet.

"Watch how you address me, bloody hell," the other snapped angrily. "For your information I'm not some blooming pansy."

It was not a very grateful response from someone who had just been rescued and for a moment Jackie nearly resorted to anger himself. As the young man got to his feet, however, Jackie's anger was swallowed up in his surprise. Without the covering of the wig, his hair was a cascade of unruly dark locks that tumbled about his face and reached to his shoulders. It would have been impossible for Jackie not to recognize the hair, the large, bright eyes, separated by a long, almost hawk-like nose, and the pouty curve of the mouth.

"Dingo Stark!" Jackie exclaimed in amazement. It was an unlikely place in which to be meeting the world famous rock-and-roll singer. He remembered reading somewhere that the young Englishman was visiting in the country but the gay bar they were outside of was not a place Jackie would have suspected as a part of his itinerary.

"Not so blooming loud," Stark warned him, glancing anxiously about. "I don't want to be recognized around this place."

"That explains the wig," Jackie said, in a lower voice. "And it's none of my business what you're doing here. But I don't need to tell you those boys meant business. One of them was pulling a knife when I came up."

"Yes, I know." Stark looked back at him now and managed what Jackie assumed was a grateful smile. "I owe you a vote of thanks, mate."

"That's all right," Jackie assured him, accepting the hand that was offered. "In a manner of speaking, protecting people is my business."

Stark raised an eyebrow. "Well, now, that's interesting, isn't it? I'd say at the moment that I might need a bit of protecting."

Jackie shook his head, "To be honest, I don't think you fall into my category. Speaking bluntly,

11

I'm usually concerned with helping out homosexuals."

"I see." Stark did not seem at all dissuaded by the statement. "As a matter of fact, that sounds all the more interesting. Tell me, Mr....?"

"Holmes, Jackie Holmes. Call me Jackie."

"Tell me, Jackie, would you be interested in running up to my hotel with me? I have a feeling we might be able to do a little business together."

Jackie hesitated for a moment, remembering the redhead, Bob, who by now was probably growing very impatient. He hated giving up the prospect of a torrid session, most especially since he couldn't look forward to one with his new companion. Stark was not especially good looking, and yet there was something about him that was wildly attractive, especially when he was in action. Singing at the top of his lungs, his long hair flying about as he flailed his guitar and gyrated his narrow hips, Stark exuded an animal magnetism and vitality that set millions of young girls, and boys, afire. Too bad, Jackie thought quickly, that he was straight. On the other hand, this was business, and if there was a homosexual element involved, it was definitely right down his alley.

"Come on," he said, reaching a decision. "I'll drive you to your hotel."

* * * * * *

"This is it," Jackie said when they reached his car in the lot.

Stark stared at the vehicle in amazement. "I say, it is a wild-looking thing isn't it?"

12

The roadster before them was finished in a pale shade of blue. The color, however, was the only docile thing about the car's appearance. High cycle fenders arched gracefully over the huge wire wheels, encasing the side-mounted spare and reaching down and back to the wide running boards that were typically Italian, high off the ground.

"Alfa Romeo," Jackie explained as they climbed inside. "1925 vintage, a 22-90 RLSS model."

The six-cylinder, three-liter engine sprang to life. Jackie struggled with the four speed gearbox, a hard one to handle, and swung out of the parking lot at a fast clip. Despite its age and size the car was easy to handle, the steering quick and precise, the performance surprisingly muscular.

"Noisy brute, isn't it?" Stark commented, enjoying the cool night winds that whipped over him.

"That it is. By the way, I hope you are not wearing rubber sole shoes."

"I'm not," Stark assured him, giving him a puzzled look. "But why do you ask?"

Jackie nodded his head down, toward the aluminum footboard. "It gets hot. First time I drove it, I wore rubber sole shoes and the damned thing melted the soles."

Ahead of them a compact car pulled out from a side street. Jackie swore aloud and slammed his foot on the brake. The result was a blood-curdling howl from the wheels. Despite the noise, however, the action did rather little to stop the car. They came within inches of the compact before the frightened driver of that car, unnerved by the racket and the sight of the classic roadster roaring down upon him, finally accelerated out of their path.

Stark had turned somewhat paler. "What was all that about?" he asked finally.

Jackie giggled. "They hadn't yet invented modern braking systems at the time this car was built. These are four-wheel brakes, but there are no linings. The noise you heard was the sound of cast iron shoes rubbing directly against the steel of the drums. Added to that, there's an intricate system of chain, cable and steel tapes that was intended to transmit the pressure of your foot to the brake drums. By the time it does its work, you've usually hit whatever you were trying to miss."

"I see," Stark answered, in a none too enthusiastic tone.

If the rock-and-roll singer's nerves had been rather abused by the peculiarities of the car, he had yet to suffer still more hardship. They had gone only a few blocks more when, with a gush of a small waterfall, the dash panel erupted before him. The seams gave way suddenly to release a river of warm oil over his lap.

Jackie brought the car to as hasty a stop as the braking system would allow, unable to suppress the gales of laughter that left him shaking.

"It's not bloody funny," Stark roared, viewing the results of the accident.

"Sorry," Jackie apologized, growing more sober as he produced rags from beneath the seat and began mopping up the oil that had all but inundated his companion.

"I should have suspected trouble. The car has two oil tanks, one under the dash and the crankcase itself. The idea is to fill the dash tank, which automatically feeds the engine. I left my mechanic to service the car and he must have mistakenly filled both tanks. The overtaxed seams just gave up."

Despite his ministrations to the other's lap, which had been deliberately quite thorough, and more enjoyable for Jackie than for Stark, the damage to the slacks Stark was wearing was irreparable.

"I'll see that they are replaced," Jackie assured him. "And I am sorry, really."

Stark was still shaken and not particularly cheerful. "Are there any more booby traps set to spring?" he wanted to know.

"I give you my word," Jackie promised, starting off again.

To their mutual relief they reached Stark's hotel without further incident. Jackie was surprised to note that it was not a particularly outstanding hotel.

As though divining his thoughts, Stark explained. "It's difficult to make myself inconspicuous," he said as they entered the lobby. "But there are times when I simply have to get away from the fans who are always trying to tear me apart. So far, no one has discovered me here but I wouldn't have had a minute's peace in the Hilton."

The hotel employees regarded them with amusement and curiosity as Stark passed through the small lobby in his oil-stained trousers. For an answer, Stark only glowered at each one in turn. He was still glowering when they reached his room.

"I think I'll feel better if I get out of these," he said. "And take a good shower. Can you make yourself at home?"

"Don't hurry," Jackie assured him, seating himself on one edge of the bed. "I'll be here when you finish."

He did not attempt to hide his interest as Stark undressed, dropping the trousers rather noisily into the wastebasket. To his disappointment Stark donned a terry cloth robe before removing his underpinnings. Jackie had seen enough of the body, however, to know that it was a nice one, long-limbed and sturdy.

He remembered as Stark disappeared into the bathroom that the young man had not always been a highly paid singer. He had come from one of the rougher districts of London and if one were to believe the publicity biographies, his early life had been a hard one.

Only two years before Stark had been a construction worker living with his large family in a crowded and shabby apartment. His two years of success had apparently not yet softened him. He was still muscular and rugged, and the rough edges still showed through the veneer of polish he had acquired.

Stark was back quickly, his legs dripping water beneath the robe. "Now then," he said, leaning against the dresser and folding his arms over his chest. "You said that you were in the business of protection and that this involved homosexuals. Can you be more specific about this business of yours?"

Jackie hesitated briefly. He did not, as a rule, discuss his work with strangers as, for all practical purposes, Stark was. On the other hand, Stark had hinted that he needed help, and if Jackie was going to supply that help, he owed some explanation.

"I'm an agent for an organization called C.A.M.P. It's an international, underground organization dedicated to the advancement and protection of homosexuals."

"Is there a demand for such an outfit?" Stark asked, interested.

Jackie nodded. "Most definitely. No one knows just how many homosexuals there are in the world, but it's safe to say there are millions. Most of them pay a heavy price for being what they are. In most countries there are laws prohibiting homosexual acts, sometimes involving life imprisonment. Even where there are no laws there is a great deal of ignorance regarding the subject, with the resultant myths and prejudices. C.A.M.P. has numerous sections that deal with every aspect of homosexuality. Some of them work to improve the legal situation, others work in the medical and social fields, among others."

"And the protection?"

"Unfortunately, it's too often necessary. These homosexuals are frequently the victims of unscrupulous people, ranging from small time roughnecks who make a sport of queer hunting—cruising around looking for homosexuals to molest—to blackmailers and sometimes worse. There's little police protection for the homosexual. Remember, he's technically outside the law anyway. That's where I come in. My section works as a police agency for homosexuals everywhere, whenever needed."

"I see," Stark said thoughtfully, rubbing his chin with his hand.

"But I'm not sure I see what your interest in all this is," Jackie said frankly. "You were pretty blunt in stating that you weren't, as you put it, a pansy."

A slight blush tinged the angular face pink. "I'm not, of course," Stark agreed. "But I think I can qualify for your services, Jackie."

"In what way?" Jackie asked, puzzled.

Stark was becoming more embarrassed as he talked and his reluctance was apparent in the fact that he looked away from Jackie as he went on slowly.

"These blackmailers you mentioned," he explained, stammering. "I know all about that aspect of the problem. You see, I've just found myself confronted with the same situation. To be brief about it, I'm being blackmailed. At least, someone is *trying* to blackmail me."

Jackie leaned forward on the edge of the bed, definitely interested. Stark, so famous now as to be almost a household word and earning a phenomenal salary, would be a ripe target for any blackmailer.

"What are they blackmailing you for?" he asked, still curious about how this was connected with him and his work for C.A.M.P.

Stark's face went from pink to a deep crimson red. "It's over some homosexual incidents," he managed to stammer.

♠ CHAPTER TWO ♠
λ

Jackie's interest and his curiosity were aroused still further by the statement. "Isn't that a little contradictory," he asked.

"I suppose I'd better tell you the whole story," Stark agreed with obvious discomfort. "When I said I wasn't homosexual I was being honest. But isn't it true that most blokes go through a stage of that as children?"

"That's true enough," Jackie agreed. "Some experts think that the heterosexual person goes through a stage of homosexual development, which he outgrows as he grows older. According to that theory, the homosexual in a sense gets bogged down in that stage and never develops beyond it. Some people, of course, the ones they call bisexual, grow into adulthood capable of enjoying both sexes. In fact, many authorities think that everyone remains more or less bisexual, but that the conditioning in our society prohibits the average adult from practicing or even recognizing his homosexual urges."

"That's how I understood it," Stark answered. Jackie's matter-of-fact approach had eased his embarrassment somewhat. "Well, that's what it was in my case. The incidents involved were childhood incidents. They took place when I was only sixteen and seventeen."

Jackie did not interrupt to point out that the young man was not much older than that now.

"I grew up in a rough neighborhood," Stark when on. "I was pretty much of a loner, until I met Steve. He was a different sort, out of place in the neighborhood, if you know what I mean."

Jackie nodded his head. He knew how difficult life could be for the homosexual growing up in such an environment. He himself had fared better, coming from a family of vast wealth, but his work had often led him to the others.

"Steve was a nice-looking chap, but sort of delicate and fragile, if you can picture him. He was a pansy—excuse me, a homosexual—even then, and still is, so far as I know. Anyway, he had had quite a bit of experience at it, as I found out eventually.

"When I first met him, he was being worked over roundly by a bunch of ruffians. I pitched in and saved his skin. After that, he sort of attached himself to me. For me it was like having a pet dog around, or something like that, and he was a nice enough chap. Besides, I hadn't had any friends of my own and the two of us became quite close."

"How close?" Jackie prodded him when he paused, restraining himself from smiling.

"Close enough," Stark answered, blushing slightly again, "To fool around a bit with one another. Kid stuff, you understand."

How long did this go on," Jackie asked. "This fooling around between the two of you?"

"Two years. I got my big break then and left the old neighborhood."

Two years, Jackie thought, was quite a long time for a trivial affair to continue. Nor had it ended, he reminded himself, because Stark had found himself a girl or anything of that sort, but because he had moved from the neighborhood. But he thought it best to keep these thoughts to himself.

"Where is Steve now?" he asked.

"Oh, I saw that he was taken care of," Stark answered quickly, as though suspecting some implied criticism in the question. "I couldn't afford to have him stay around, at the risk of scandal, but I saw that he had enough money to take care of himself. He's living here, as a matter or fact, in this country. I haven't yet gotten in touch with him, as he'd moved from his last address."

"I see. And someone got hold of this story?"

"Yes. I don't know how, but a few days ago I got a note. It included quite a bit of information about Steve and myself, enough to make it clear that the sender knew we had been, uh, doing it together, so to speak. The note suggested that I be at the parking lot behind the bar, tonight. When I got there, I found those three toughies. They put it on the line: one hundred thousand dollars in your money, or they'd ruin my career by spreading the story about me. I lost my temper and took a swing at one of them. You know the rest."

Jackie nodded grimly. "I'd say you are in a spot."

"I don't suppose there's much that can be done now," Stark said. "After I lost my temper and started a fight, they're sure to start their smear campaign."

"I don't think so. It's the money they want, and chances are good they'll try again, after you've had time to cool off."

"Is there anything your outfit, C.A.M.P., can do to help me? I can't go to the police, of course, without risking the same exposure."

"We can try," Jackie answered. "There's not much to go on. Did you save the note?"

Stark shook his head glumly. "I tore it up. But it wouldn't have helped much. It was all printed on plain paper. It was left under my door here."

"At least we got a look at those three who met you tonight," Jackie pointed out hopefully. "I may get a lead there, if I can identify them."

"There's one thing more that worries me," Stark said quietly.

"What's that?"

"I've kept a sort of diary, most of my life," Stark explained. "I used to write down things that happened to me and how I felt about them. It's got everything about Steve in it, every single time we were together, and everything we did, in detail, in my own handwriting."

Jackie groaned aloud. "Don't tell me our friends have that in their possession?"

"No, thank heaven for that," Stark assured him quickly. "I have it here, with me. But I've been scared green that they might get hold of it. They could sell that for a fortune and ruin my career in the bargain."

"I think," Jackie said, standing. "I'd better take that with me, just to be on the safe side. You have my word that I won't read it, of course, but I think it will be safer at my office than here."

"You're right, of course," Stark agreed. He took a key from atop his dresser and unlocked his suitcase, removing a thick, battered notebook from it. "I suppose I should have burned it," he said, handing the book to Jackie. "But somehow I couldn't bring myself to do that."

"I'll take care of it," Jackie assured him. "And don't worry, we'll put an end to this scheme."

"I'll pay a fee, of course," Stark told him with a grateful smile. "And I'll be in your debt forever."

"Forget it," Jackie answered, "It's our job, remember. We don't base our assistance on whether or not someone can afford us."

"You know," Stark said after a pause, a faint smile playing across the deep red of his lips. "When I look back on it, those incidents with Steve were sort of pleasant. Nothing serious, of course, but I can't deny that I enjoyed them."

"At least you're more honest about that than many others," Jackie said. He was puzzled by the change he could not quite define.

"I wonder," Stark said, his smile broadening although the blush had returned. "If any one of us ever really outgrows his childhood?"

Jackie was beginning to understand at last. The gleam that had crept into Stark's dark eyes, the timid blush—unless he was badly mistaken, and he rarely was about such things, the rock-and-roll singer, idol of millions, was making a pass at him.

"Are you suggesting," he asked quietly, "That I make you a child again, just for tonight?"

Stark held his ground and met the questioning eyes squarely, despite his embarrassment. "I've never dared to repeat those scenes, because of the risk. But I know I can trust you and, well, it might be a bit of fun, mightn't it?"

Jackie grinned broadly. It was natural, even among the most sophisticated, to retain a certain awe for stars of such magnitude as Dingo Stark. Everyone had some idol of whom they would cherish a souvenir: a lock of hair, a piece of clothing. In his own case the memory of a bedtime romp was the sort of souvenir Jackie most enjoyed. And after all, there was that redhead that he stood up to come here, a tempting morsel he had hated to pass up.

"It might be at that," he agreed, laying the diary gently atop the dresser. He did not hesitate as he began to remove his clothing. His schedule was frequently a busy one and more often than not such diversions as this had to be accomplished with speed and efficiency.

"Would you—would you like the light off?" Stark asked, no longer the self-assured singer star, but an awkward, uncertain young man.

"I always believe one should see what one is buying," Jackie answered. "Besides, I'm not bashful."

He had, in fact, no reason to be modest over the body that was coming into view. Dressed, and assuming his customary manner, the youthful blond gave an impression of being weak and even effeminate. He was small and slender but the more than casual observer, seeing the body naked, could at once see that weakness was only an illusion.

Beneath the delicate-looking skin, well-trained and coordinated muscles rippled and surged as he moved. It had often proven to his advantage to appear less than an athlete but Jackie was that and more. At his command were phenomenal resources of strength and agility that had seen him through more than one fracas.

His body was nearly hairless, except for a bloom of golden silk at the base of his abdomen that framed a more than ample manhood and the soft down that gave added luster to the curving softness of his buttocks.

"Tell me," he addressed his companion as he stepped nearer. "Those gyrations you use when you're singing—did you learn those from Steve?"

"Some of them," Stark admitted shyly. With his eyes he had been devouring the attractive body, now naked before him.

Jackie took the robe gently in his hands, pulling it open. Stark's body lived up to its promises. He was tall and big-boned, with an exaggerated angularity that was not pretty but at the same time uniquely attractive. His chest was not particularly developed, and his waist rather thick in contrast to his slender hips, with the result that his shape was nearly straight up and down.

The same dark hair that framed his face was repeated thickly at the center of his chest, thinning out to encircle the deep rosettes of his flat, masculine nipples. From his navel the luxuriant growth began again, fanning over his gently rounded abdomen to climax at his thighs and continue down the long columns of his legs.

Looking down, Jackie was pleased to discover that his nudity had not been wasted on the English youth. Nor had he any reason to be disappointed by what he saw. The young Steve, Jackie decided, had had more than one reason for encouraging and continuing the relationship with his comrade. A homosexual, even an active and experienced one, could shop around quite a bit without finding better.

Stark shivered slightly as Jackie lifted the robe off the wide shoulders and tugged it gently from the arms, letting it fall to the floor.

"Nervous?" he asked tenderly.

"A little," Stark answered.

Jackie led him to the bed, flicking off the light as they lowered themselves to its surface. His own ardor had been aroused by the ripened fruits before him, waiting to be plucked. At the moment he could not help resenting Stark's young friend. He would like to have been the first himself.

He did not attempt to kiss the face near his, although their lips were only inches apart. He knew Stark's type. The ones who did not regard themselves as homosexual were sometimes receptive to a little "fun", but more often than not they drew the line at kissing a member of their own sex. It was a peculiarity that Jackie recognized, although he found it difficult to understand.

Stark had no such reluctance, however, in the use of his body. His embrace was warm and eager, his body twisting and squirming as he crushed it tightly against Jackie's. His hands played up and down Jackie's back, reaching to fondle and knead the yielding softness of the taut mounds at the base of Jackie's torso. For several minutes they twisted and rubbed together, sweating with the warmth of their passion.

Jackie smiled to himself as he recognized the preliminaries to the method Stark expected to use, a method known to some as the "Princeton rub" because of its alleged popularity among the students of that school, and to more serious researchers as the English Method. The latter name came from the reportedly common use of the method among English boarding school students, although the Greeks, who called it *merizein*, were said to have practiced the same method in their highly homosexual civilization.

In its simplest form, the method was little more than a prolonged embrace, the participants pressed tightly against one another's abdomen until the finish.

It was not a technique that Jackie frequently employed but he had long since discarded any inhibitions that he might have possessed, devoting himself instead to giving and deriving pleasure by whatever means preferred by his partner. If this was what it took to please the lanky young man in his arms he was happy to oblige. He reached for his companion, moistening the taut flesh with saliva.

For himself, his own pleasure was heightened by the obvious delight that Stark took in the caress. The English youth was beside himself with passion, the muscles of his hips taut as he pushed upward, his sliding, heaving stomach providing the physical stimulation for Jackie.

As his ardor soared Stark grew more abandoned, his hands clawing at Jackie's body, his teeth
scraping the flesh of Jackie's shoulder. Jackie
stroked and fondled his partner all the while, bringing into play his thorough knowledge of the male
body. Stark was still quite young and the erogenous
zones of a young man, he knew, were not unlike
those of a girl.

His ministrations produced soft moans of delight and he wondered, as his hands explored Stark's
firm, voluptuous buttocks, causing Stark to shudder
convulsively, if the enterprising Steve might not
have introduced Stark to other techniques as well.
That, however, was a question hopefully to be explored on some subsequent occasion.

The session was proving to be a brief one, for
both of them were rapidly approaching their peak.
Jackie would have liked to linger, prolong the excitement, but he was already too far gone to slow
down and the labored breathing near his ear told
him that Stark was in the same condition.

They clung tightly to one another, gasping
and panting, and Jackie's belly was suddenly
flooded with Stark's warm moistness. He answered
it in kind; the two on them drenched with the success of their actions.

"Time for another shower," Stark said finally.
In the pale light that filtered through the window, he
was smiling up at Jackie, no longer shy and awkward.

"I'll join you," Jackie agreed, standing and
offering his companion a hand.

They shared a long, stimulating shower together, affectionately soaping one another's backs

and taking frequent time out for horseplay. Stark seemed even younger than his years, a carefree young man playfully happy with someone he liked, and Jackie was not sorry he had promised to help him.

They left the shower finally. Stark donned his robe and watched with regretful eyes as Jackie dressed.

"Was I...?" Stark hesitated, dropping his eyes shyly, "Was I all right?"

"You were great," Jackie reassured him, retrieving the diary from the dresser. "I hope you aren't suffering any regrets."

Stark shook his head and looked up again. "No, it was even more fun than I remembered with Steve."

"Maybe we can try it again," Jackie said hopefully. "I think Steve neglected a few points. Maybe I can show you some of them."

Stark was timid again. "We'll see. I don't know if I want to. Not that I didn't like it, but I'm wondering if I didn't like it too much."

Jackie left the statement unchallenged. This was always a hard thing for some males to face and many of them preferred to take the easy course by foregoing what, to their way of thinking, were sinful pleasures.

"I'll be in touch," Jackie told him, opening the door into the hall. "As soon as I can learn anything. And I'll look after these memoirs for you."

He paused, smiling, and added, "It's too bad you won't get to record tonight in it."

"I'll add it when this is all over," Stark told him. "And don't worry, I won't be likely to forget any of the details."

Jackie grinned broadly and went out, closing the door after himself. Singing, he decided as he went down in the elevator, was far from the only talent Dingo Stark possessed. All in all, he couldn't really regret missing his rendezvous with the redhead from the bar. Anyway it was likely he would see the redhead again. Stark, however, might not be in the same mood the next time.

The Alfa Romeo was waiting for him across the street.

With the diary under his arm, Jackie started toward it. Behind him there was the sound of running feet. The alarm sounded in his mind a split second too late. He tried to duck but his attacker was faster.

He head seemed to explode with the burst of fireworks that dimmed quickly into an impenetrable blackness as he fell to the sidewalk.

♠ <u>CHAPTER THREE</u> ♠
λ

He came to slowly, his head throbbing painfully. Memory swept over him and he opened his eyes, shaking his head to shrug off the clinging blackness.

He was lying on the sidewalk. His watch informed him that he had not been out for long after all, no more than a few minutes. There was no sign of his attacker, however, who had had ample time to make a getaway.

He remembered the diary finally and bolted to his feet, his eyes sweeping the sidewalk about him. It was gone, of course. The book had been the reason for the bump on his head. No doubt the blackmailers had their eye on this place. They might even have heard his parting comment to Dingo, regarding the "memoirs," or they might somehow have already known about them. In any event they now had in their hands the most powerful tool they could use against Stark, a guaranteed fortune, if not from Stark, then from some unscrupulous publisher who would pay handsomely for the handwritten and scandalous document.

Stark would have to be told, of course. Jackie considered returning to the hotel room but decided instead to allow his new friend a few minutes of peace. There would be time enough to phone him later, from his office. He climbed into the roadster and drove away, piloting the car with grim reckless-ness.

He reached the downtown area of Hollywood, making his way down the famed Hollywood Boule-vard, past theaters of pseudo-oriental design and offbeat nightspots. Multiple streams of cars moved by on either side, crowding together as the nighttime activity of the area rushed toward its peak.

Twin figures of light, klieg lights for some "grand opening" in the city, probed the sky over-head. The sidewalks were crowded with pedestrians. Among them, obvious homosexuals strolled up and down, casting hungry eyes upon one another.

Young men, some of them scarcely more than children, stood or walked, their trousers bulging with lewd displays of the wares they offered to any and all purchasers. It was a city of cars and search-lights, and furtive-eyed males, a Mecca for the ho-mosexual.

It was a city too of stars, some of whom would soar high into the sky, flaming brilliantly. Of-ten the brilliance would be brief, the fall sudden. For some of them the fall would result from a brief mo-ment of indiscretion. For Dingo Stark, whose flame was at its zenith now, it had been two years.

Where had they met for their clandestine ad-ventures, those two youths of London—on rooftops, perhaps, or in parks? How often, and with what tenderness had they clung together, perhaps even with genuine affection? And those two years now threatened to extinguish Stark's career, unless Jackie could somehow prevent it from happening.

Jackie turned off the boulevard, making his way a few blocks down a street, then across another. At last a faded neon proclaimed the location of the Round-Up, one of the many bars in the city that provided a refuge for the homosexuals, and one of the least glamorous.

Jackie parked outside, grimacing at the howl of the brakes, and entered the bar. The patrons here, and there were a surprising number of them, were the less discreet, the less careful, members of the homosexual society. No one here was likely to snicker, or sniff coolly, at the appearance or behavior of anyone else.

Jackie went past the bar to the rear. Beyond a musty drape he entered a short hallway and finally the room marked MEN.

To his disappointment there was someone in the room. Another time he would have gone on by the cold white fixtures that stood at the wall. Now he would have to pretend, and stall for time until the stranger left. Fumbling with his trousers, Jackie stepped up to the receptacle.

It was not an unpleasant diversion. At least he was treated to a view of exposed flesh that would ordinarily have aroused his interest, but he had other things on his mind now. He looked up, recognizing the question in the eyes that studied him. He smiled apologetically and shook his head. The stranger shrugged, and stepped back from the wall. A minute later he was gone.

Jackie too went toward the door, opening it and allowing it to swing closed as though he had left. Then, crouching low, he retraced his steps toward the rear of the restroom. He knew that the mirror along the wall was a two-way affair, and beyond it a member of the local vice squad watched the room for any homosexual activity. It was a form of entrapment common to the local police and for this reason Jackie remained below the line of vision afforded by the mirror.

He reached the second of the two enclosed stalls provided, one bearing an OUT OF ORDER sign on the door. Stepping inside, he slid away the top of the water closet and put his hand into the water, feeling for a concealed button. A second later the wall slid open. He stepped inside. The panel closed after him and a second door opened on to a spacious and luxurious living room.

This was one of the many offices of C.A.M.P., the one from which he most frequently worked. Here, in one of the rooms beyond this one, was an elaborate accumulation of electronic equipment beyond description, one of the centers from which C.A.M.P. conducted its activities. The equipment was related and linked to the nerve center of High Camp, their highly secret and efficient headquarters.

He was met by a towering giant of a man, a six-foot-five-inch figure, handsome in a bullish, muscle-bulging way.

"Hi, Rich," Jackie greeted him, closing the second panel after himself.

Rich returned the greeting, not in the least surprised by Jackie's arrival. Indeed, there was no reason for him to be surprised, as Jackie well knew. A large and detailed map of the city of Los Angeles and the surrounding areas dominated one of the walls of the inner office. At the moment a red dot of light would be shining on the map, at the exact location of this room, because he was here. The light was a signal from the miniature homing device imbedded in an artificial thumbnail Jackie wore on one hand. Day and night, wherever he went, the light followed his movements on the map, showing his exact location at all times. He might be out of touch with C.A.M.P. occasionally but C.A.M.P. was never out of touch with him.

"You look sore," Rich commented, pouring a drink for the blond agent.

"I am," Jackie told him. "Mentally and physically."

"What's up?" Rich asked.

Jackie seated himself at a sofa before the fireplace and tasted his drink, nodding his approval. He described the fight that he had interrupted earlier. When he said who he had rescued Rich's eyes widened.

"Dingo Stark! Did you get his autograph?" Rich asked.

Jackie smiled faintly. "I don't know if you could call it that, exactly," he answered.

Rich frowned and grew silent again. Jackie knew that the dark giant felt more than a little affection for him and he knew that Rich was always slightly hurt to know that Jackie engaged in sexual combat with someone else. For his own part however, Jackie had never tried to pretend he was any different from what he was. Variety, in his case, was virtually a necessity and although he was admittedly fond of Rich he knew he could never give up his pursuit of other conquests.

He went on, explaining the rest of the evening, although omitting the more intimate activities. His story held Rich's attention throughout.

"And they got the diary after all," Rich asked when Jackie had finished.

"They got the diary and I got a lump on the head," Jackie assured him, rubbing the spot gingerly.

"You're right, it sounds like a job for C.A.M.P.," Rich agreed.

"More than that," Jackie said, "I have a personal score to settle now. I gave my word that I'd keep that book safe and I failed. I intend to get it back before it causes any harm."

"Where do we start?" Rich asked, standing as though preparing to go into action at once. He was not, like Jackie, an outside agent. His job was to man the office, to provide Jackie with whatever form of assistance or protection he needed when working on any case.

Jackie frowned thoughtfully. "I'm going to have to call Dingo Stark and tell him the bad news. But I have a hunch there's more involved than just one star's career. This sounds to me like a careful, well-planned setup, something done on a big scale."

"Could be a blackmail ring, maybe," Rich said, nodding. "I'll see what we have on file that might give us any clues."

He left the room, heading for the inner office. Reluctantly Jackie crossed to the phone at the desk. The phone was little more than an extra extension of the one in his own apartment, one of many precautions. If ever a call should be traced by anyone it would lead him to Jackie's apartment rather than to this secret office.

Stark sounded as though he had been asleep when he answered the phone. He was instantly alert, however, as Jackie identified himself and began to explain about the loss of the diary.

Stark took it calmly, considering the implications the news held for him.

"Do you think you can get it back?" he asked over the phone.

"I'm going to," Jackie assured him.

There was a brief pause. "I'll be very grateful if you can," Stark said finally, in a lower voice. "I think you know what I mean."

Despite his low spirits, Jackie smiled at the receiver. He knew only too well just how grateful the singer star could be. If he had needed a reward to encourage his efforts, Stark had picked exactly the right one to offer.

"I'll get it back," he said firmly.

Rich was back in the room within a few minutes, carrying a small stack of papers, the information that had been hurriedly relayed to him from the files of High Camp.

"Looks like we may have something here," he said, handing the reports over to Jackie. "High Camp's very interested in this matter. In case there was any doubt in your mind you're assigned to look into it thoroughly. I'm to assist."

"Good, I have a personal interest in this one," Jackie told him. He began to read through the brief reports, his lips moving wordlessly as he read. "Interesting. A suicide here in Los Angeles, prominent banker, no logical reason for the suicide, except that our files listed him as a homosexual. Prior to his death, six weeks ago he was known to have spent large sums of money, although the expenditures were never traced."

He turned to the next report. "Movie actress, just starting on her way up to the top. Contract canceled after scandal regarding her Lesbian activities. Devotes her time to drinking since then."

The third report was even more interesting. "Prominent San Francisco architect, another suicide. Police found some evidence of a blackmail, possibly involving homosexual activities."

He turned to the fourth and last report. "What's this one? High level diplomat retires in Washington. Oh yes, he had recently visited the San Francisco area. No reason given for his retirement. C.A.M.P. suspects he may have been engaged in occasional homosexual activities."

"It does look big," he said, looking up at Rich. "This could all be coincidence of course. Or it could be the trail of a full-fledged and top-level blackmail ring preying on those who are not only especially vulnerable with a lot to lose but can afford to pay highly."

"And operating out of this area," Rich offered. "Or out of San Francisco."

Jackie was thoughtful for a moment, glancing back over the reports. "More likely San Francisco," he said.

He stood abruptly and went to the phone, once again calling the hotel at which Dingo Stark was staying under another name. This time Stark did not sound as though he had been asleep. Poor fellow, Jackie thought sympathetically, he's probably been sitting there worrying about that diary.

"I haven't been to San Francisco in years," Stark answered his question. "Just once, on a tour early in my career."

Jackie left the number of his apartment where Stark could reach him if anything came up and hung up the phone again. "Nothing here," he announced. "That actress, Chris Langley. She's still alive and if she was being blackmailed we might convince her to tell us about it. Get me a current address on her. I'll contact her in the morning."

"What about the three who were working over Stark when you arrived? Can you identify any of them?"

"I was just getting to that. Let's have a look at the files on blackmailers, see if any of them look familiar."

It was already well after midnight and it would take hours for even a hurried examination of the extensive files maintained by C.A.M.P. Both men, however, had long since accustomed themselves to keeping inconvenient hours. Sleep was a luxury when they were working on a case.

Jackie seated himself again on the sofa while Rich opened a special cabinet nearby, operating switches. A minute later the lights dimmed and the wall opposite began to glow. A large double picture of a face, not unlike the mug shots employed by police, appeared on the wall.

"Nope," Jackie said quickly. The next face appeared and produced the same comment.

For two hours he studied face after face, rejecting some of them quickly, examining others for a few minutes before giving the negative answer.

"Hold onto that one," he said finally. He scowled and studied the picture before him. "It was dark," he said. "And I didn't have much time to look them over. But he looks like one of them."

The next hour was uneventful. At last, however, Jackie sat forward excitedly. "That one," he said quickly and without uncertainty. "That's the big brute, the ape I told you about."

They went on, studying the remaining files, without any further success. When they were finished the lights came up again and the wall returned to its normal appearance.

"I'll check these two out," Rich told him. He took the slides with him into the inner office. Here their code numbers would be fed into a transmitter, forwarded to High Camp. Within minutes they would have all of the information that was on file regarding the two suspects.

While they waited for the reply Rich brought coffee for the both of them and they sat in silence, individually contemplating the situation. A soft tinkle of chimes, much like the glass wind chimes of the Orient—although there was no movement of the air in the apartment—announced the answer from High Camp.

Rich was grim when he again entered the room. He handed the reports to Jackie wordlessly.

Jackie whistled softly as he looked them over. "Jack Savage," he read aloud. "Small time blackmailer and con man for many years. Bruno Scotto, one time strong-arm man for the Green Bay Gang, notorious queer-hater, one time suspect in the slaying of a homosexual. Both now believed working for B.U.T.C.H."

He raised his eyes solemnly to Rich's. It was a name with which they were both familiar: B.U.T.C.H., Brothers United to Crush Homosexuality. Like C.A.M.P. it was an underground organization, although it had as its goal the harassment and destruction of homosexuality. Their tools included vice and crime of every sort, and their agents were everywhere. Often a homosexual, particularly one who gave the appearance of wealth, would pick up some lovely young male and enjoy a session of romance, only to find himself the victim of blackmail and worse. Among the unsolved murders of homosexuals in the files of C.A.M.P., all but a few were believed to be the work of B.U.T.C.H.

"The big boys," Rich said softly.

"And getting bigger, it seems," Jackie said. "In the past their blackmail activities have been random, accidental things. But this looks like they've entered the field on a large scale, seeking out the biggest targets for their filthy trap."

"They're elusive," Rich reminded him. "And they play rough."

"So do I," Jackie said coldly. He had tangled with B.U.T.C.H. on more than one occasion. Thus far the score had remained even: a few wins for him, a few for them. The headquarters, the core of their operations, remained as yet undiscovered, although the operation was suspected to be as widespread and extensive as C.A.M.P.

Jackie returned the reports and stood, finishing off the last of his coffee. "I'd better get back to my own apartment," he declared, taking a moment to glance at the last report, the one showing the address of Chris Langley.

"It's almost morning," Rich told him gently. "Why don't you sleep here for an hour or so?"

Jackie smiled gratefully, reading the affection in the large dark eyes. It would be wonderful to lie in those giant arms, to afford one another a brief interlude of sex. But for now he had work to think of.

"When this is over," he said, giving Rich's cheek a gentle pat. "I promise you a toss in the hay like you've never had."

He started from the room. "Oh, by the way," he said, turning back. "I had some trouble with the Alfa. Have one of the boys from Mechanics pick it up and look it over, will you? I'll take a cab home."

"Nothing bad I hope."

Jackie smiled despite his grim mood, remembering the spilled oil. It had given him a chance to rub Stark's lap thoroughly and maybe start the wheels turning in Stark's mind. And if it hadn't been for the oil, Stark would not have shed his clothes and showered and donned a robe—which had been so easy to take off, before there was time for a change of heart.

"No, I guess you couldn't call it bad," he said, leaving.

♠ CHAPTER FOUR ♠
λ

The phone rang a little before nine the following morning. Jackie had had less than three hours' sleep, although his eyes opened at once and he reached for the instrument as he sat up. The voice on the other end was Dingo Stark's.

"Just thought I should tell you," Stark explained in a voice that indicated he too had slept little. "I learned that Steve's in San Francisco. I don't know just where yet but as soon as I get the address I'll let you know."

"Thanks," Jackie answered. "That may help." The signs were all pointing to San Francisco. In the past he had been unable to determine which city served as a headquarters for B.U.T.C.H. This lead could have implications stretching far beyond the immediate case.

He showered, standing for long minutes under a hard stream of ice-cold water to guarantee that he was awake and ready for action. While he was dressing he gulped down a steaming cup of coffee. In a short time, he was in the private elevator that carried him from his apartment to the garage in the basement.

Efficient as always, the mechanic from C.A.M.P. had already repaired the oil tank of the Alfa, and had delivered it to its stall. Jackie allowed it to warm up for a minute or two before starting out.

The boarding house at which he was to find Chris Langley was a far cry from the sort of places she must have inhabited only a few short months before. This one was definitely seedy and told more clearly than words how far and how fast she had fallen.

"She's here," the heavy-set woman who met him at the door answered his question. "But I doubt she's in condition for visitors. I'll see if she's awake." There was not much hope in her voice.

Chris Langley was indeed awake. Even from the bottom of the stairs Jackie could hear the stream of profanities that answered the landlady's knock. A second knock resulted in a crash as something, probably an empty bottle, was hurled at the door.

The landlady marched angrily back down the stairs, her nostrils flaring. "I'll not be insulted that way, not by the likes of her," she snorted. "If she's a friend of yours you're welcome to her. And you'd better see her while you can, because I vow she'll not spend another night under this roof."

Jackie took advantage of the woman's anger to climb the stairs himself. He did not knock at the door but opened it cautiously and stepped in.

Chris Langley was a beautiful girl and her beauty was the type that was not easily destroyed. She was doing a good job of it, however, judging from her appearance, and already the telltale signs were beginning to show. To make it worse she wore no make-up. In fact, she wore nothing but a bra and panties as she sprawled across the crumpled bed.

"Who the hell are you?" she demanded, trying to get to her feet. She was drunk and the attempt was a failure. She fell upon the pillows.

"Just a friend," Jackie informed her, watching carefully in case she decided to throw another bottle. "I want to talk to you."

"What about?" she asked, eyeing him suspiciously.

"About your career," he told her bluntly. "And why it was ended."

She threw back her head and started to laugh wildly. The sound ended in a choking sob. "Very funny," she sneered. "If you don't know why I was booted out of the studio, you're the only one in the country who doesn't."

"The Lesbianism? I know about that. I'm more interested in the fact that you were being blackmailed."

The statement had the hoped-for effect. This time she managed at least to sit up straight, growing sober almost instantly.

"You know about that?" she asked him in a calmer voice.

"A little," he admitted. "I'd like to know more."

She shrugged and looked around for a cigarette. Jackie lit one and carried it to her.

"Thanks," she said, exhaling the smoke through her nostrils. "What's to know? They bled me dry for almost a year. Finally I couldn't pay any more and I told them so. Two days later I was out on my can."

"Who are they?"

"I don't know," she sighed wearily. "It started with some girl, nice looking twitch, very sweet and innocent. Of course, not too innocent. She made all the plays. I was being careful, with my career and all, but she kept coming on like Gangbusters. So I gave in, took her to bed. Boom, next thing I know she's disappeared and in her place is some apelike worm with a bunch a dirty pictures."

Apelike—it could only be Bruno Scotto. "Was he the only one you ever dealt with?" he asked.

"Yeah, the only one. And always very discreetly. He'd call and tell me where to meet him. Sometimes in a park, sometimes at a movie theater. Never the same place twice."

"This all took place here, in Los Angeles?"

"Sure, where else?"

Maybe, he thought, he had been premature in thinking that all the signs pointed to San Francisco.

"Except," she added impulsively, "That I met the girl the first time in San Francisco, while I was up there for an appearance. She followed me down here though."

So he had not been mistaken after all. "Thanks," he said, preparing to leave. "I think you've told me what I want to know."

"Hey, who are you anyway," she asked again. "You with one of the studios?"

He shook his head sadly. "No sorry, just a friend, like I said."

He was gone before she had the chance to question him any further.

* * * * * * *

At the C.A.M.P. office, Rich also was up and busy at work. "Any news?" he greeted Jackie.

"Just that I'm going on a little vacation," Jackie answered, striding into the bedroom.

"A vacation?" Rich asked, following him.

"To San Francisco," Jackie explained, already opening dresser drawers. "To see if I can get myself picked up and, hopefully, blackmailed."

Frowning, Rich took a seat on the edge of the bed. "I don't like that," he argued. "We've got a man in the San Francisco area, why not let him handle it?"

"I've got a personal interest in this one, remember," Jackie pointed out. From the dresser drawer he had selected a wig, a sandy-haired affair. He laid that aside and removed his make-up kit, with which he was able to change his appearance at will.

"You'll be where I can't help you," Rich said.

Or protect me, Jackie added silently. And many times Rich's protection had saved his life, but he was not to be dissuaded. "Contact the office up there," Jackie instructed. "Fill them in on the case. I won't risk getting in touch with them of course, but it'll be comforting to know that they're keeping an eye on things."

As he talked he was working on his face with the plastic from the make-up kit. By the time he turned back to Rich he was a different person, fuller of face, somewhat older looking than before. He donned the wig and the transformation was complete.

"Also," he went on, mentally checking off the steps he had planned. "Tell them to create a front for me. Spread a few rumors around some of the bars. The name is Jackie Garden, a wealthy gentleman from a stuffy old family, terrified of scandal. I'm from New York, vacationing here on my way to San Francisco."

In a short while he was ready to leave. No one seeing him walk toward his car would have suspected that the conservatively handsome man and the pretty blond who had left it a short while earlier were one and the same person.

* * * * * * *

He returned briefly to his apartment to pack and change into a conservative gray suit. As the scion of a stuffy eastern family he would have to forego the more flamboyant clothes he often wore.

Sophie, his miniature white poodle, followed him about the apartment as he made ready. She was accustomed to seeing him come and go at all times but she never failed to become despondent each time he packed a bag.

He was all but ready when the phone rang. Again it was Dingo Stark, this time only calling to see if there was any news.

"Nothing yet, but I'm hoping to have something for you soon," Jackie assured him.

"I'm just across the street," Stark said. "Shall I come up?"

Jackie hesitated. He was in his disguise. It could hardly do any harm however if Stark saw him like this, and the rock star was clearly despondent. "Come ahead," he answered. "But I'll have to leave for the airport in a few minutes."

Stark was there in three minutes. He stared blankly at Jackie when the door opened. "Is Jackie here?" he asked.

"I couldn't get much closer to you," Jackie said with a laugh. "Come on in."

Stark was appropriately astonished. "You? But what's all this get-up?"

"Working outfit," Jackie explained, leading the way into the apartment. "I'm on my way to San Francisco in a few minutes."

"Think you're on to something?" Stark asked.

They stopped as Sophie, spotting the stranger, sprang from the chair in which she had been dozing and bared her teeth menacingly.

"Sit, Sophie," Jackie told her sharply. The dog seated herself obediently.

"Is she really dangerous?" Stark asked, staring at the harmless looking ball of white fluff.

"Trained to kill," Jackie explained matter-of-factly. "In my business you can't have too much protection around."

Stark skirted the dog with new respect and took a seat.

"How about some coffee?" Jackie asked. At Stark's nod, he entered the kitchen and returned with two mugs of coffee.

"I'm just following up leads," he explained, seating himself. "By the way, get in touch with me as soon as you hear from your friend Steve. I'll be staying at the Essex, under the name Jackie Garden."

Sophie, having satisfied herself that the newcomer was harmless, came to where Jackie was sitting and wagged her tail energetically.

Seeing her twitching nose, Jackie took another swallow of coffee and set his cup on the floor where the dog could reach it. Sophie sniffed and gave him an icy look.

"Sorry," he said, realizing the trouble. He added a lump of sugar from the tray, stirring it, and returning it to the floor. The dog sniffed and, satisfied that it was now to her taste, lowered her snout into the cup and began to drink noisily.

"She is a bit peculiar," Stark admitted, watching the dog.

"She's mad, but sometimes useful." Jackie glanced at his watch. He would have to be on his way soon to the airport.

"I won't stay," Stark said, taking the hint. "I just wanted some reassurance. I start my personal appearances in two days and I was hoping maybe this could be straightened out by then."

"Not unless we're lucky," Jackie said. Then, seeing the disappointment on the other's face, he smiled and added, "I'll do my best."

Stark paused on their way to the door, to study the large wood carving atop the credenza. Nearly two feet tall, it was a faithful and at the same time beautiful representation of a particular portion of the male anatomy.

"What on earth...?" he stammered, embarrassed and amused at the same time.

"A trophy from C.A.M.P.," Jackie explained. "For my work."

"What are all the scratches?" Both sides of the enormous phallus were lined with deep gouges.

Jackie grinned. "To be honest, I think you'd call them notches."

"Notches?" Stark blushed. "You mean...?"

"Conquests is the nice word," Jackie answered him.

"I'd say you've been busy," Stark said quietly, continuing on toward the door.

"A little," Jackie agreed. His eyes dropped to the buttocks enclosed in the trousers before him as Stark walked toward the door. Halfway conquests didn't earn a notch. It was too bad, he thought, that he was on his way to catch a plane. He might have been able to complete the job.

THE MAN FROM C.A.M.P.

♠ CHAPTER FIVE ♠
λ

Jackie boarded the PSA jet with minutes to spare. The plane was not crowded and he took a window seat, sliding his briefcase underneath.

A minute later an attractive blond entered the plane also, starting down the aisle. Jackie gave the newcomer an admiring once over. He was in his mid-twenties and the possessor of the babyish type prettiness that helped one to look young for a few years and then, sometimes it seemed almost overnight, began treacherously adding to one's years instead. In his teens, his soft, fleshy body, not so much plump as the type described as "cuddly," and his cute round face had no doubt given him a beauty not possessed by his more gangly contemporaries. He had passed his peak and in a few years the soft curves would turn to fat. At thirty he would be unattractive. For the moment, however, there was enough left of the youthful cherub to make him appealing.

"Is this seat taken?" he asked, pausing near Jackie.

"Not at all," Jackie assured him. Fortunately, he added silently. There was nothing like an attractive companion to make a trip more pleasant.

The blond fastened his belt as the plane prepared to take off. They roared down the runway and were soon climbing upward, the California coast and the ocean dividing the scenery between them.

"You from San Francisco?" his companion asked when they were at last able to undo the seat belts.

"No, New York," Jackie answered, sticking to his assumed role. "I'm Jackie Garden."

"Bruce," his new friend introduced himself. "Bruce Hamilton."

They ordered cocktails from the stewardess. Jackie welcomed the opportunity to talk. In the first place he was always grateful for the company of an attractive male. After all, he might have spare time while in San Francisco. In the second place it was a good opportunity to spread the word of his arrival, hopefully so that it would reach the right ears. If B.U.T.C.H. was operating out of San Francisco and looking for rich, vulnerable people to blackmail, the details he was providing to his companion should be of interest to them.

"Tell me," Bruce asked at one point, in a low voice, "are you gay?"

Jackie started as though embarrassed and frightened by the remark and glanced nervously around, but there was no one close enough to hear. "I don't think I want to discuss that here," he whispered. "It's a dangerous question for one in my position."

"Don't tell me you work for the government or something?" Bruce asked him, surprised and a little amused by the tone of secrecy.

"No, nothing like that. But mother…well, you have no idea to what lengths she would go to avoid scandal. That's why I'm here, you see. I don't dare, well, let my hair down back home. So once or twice a year I get out of town and have a little fun. But even so I have to be very careful."

"Seems to me like a lonely way to live," Bruce decided. "I can't imagine how you'd manage to have any fun."

Jackie shrugged and sighed sadly. "If I'm lucky, I meet some nice young man and spend my time with him. I'm afraid I wasn't lucky enough to meet anyone is Los Angeles."

"Where are you staying in San Francisco?"

"At the Essex," Jackie said. He wondered briefly if he had a nibble. Bruce, however, did not seem eager to take advantage of any opportunities the conversation afforded.

"Maybe we can get together for a drink while you're in town," Bruce suggested in the offhand way that suggested they would probably not see one another again.

* * * * * * *

The flight was not a long one. Less than an hour after takeoff they were landing in San Francisco. "Can I give you a lift anywhere?" Bruce offered.

Jackie was tempted, for personal reasons. He would like to have cultivated a brief friendship with the curvy blond, but it seemed unlikely that Bruce would be any help to his work and that was his first consideration.

"No thanks, I'll just hop into a cab," he answered. "But I'll look forward to that call."

He found a cab and was driven into town to the expensive and long established Essex House, just right for the conservative sort of visitor.

He had some time yet before dinner. After dinner he would have to start making himself discreetly conspicuous. If C.A.M.P. had planted their rumors successfully, there were already whispers around town about the fabulously wealthy gentleman who was visiting. With luck he would not have to work too hard to make contact. The interested parties would do that for him.

He had time before dinner to see a little of the city, one of his favorite places. The air was brisk, the city alive with activity. The colorful cable cars, clanging and clattering, made their way laboriously up Powell Street, straining themselves as they climbed the steep hills. There was a vague scent of the ocean everywhere. Smartly dressed women and groups of sailors elbowed one another on the sidewalks.

Jackie allowed himself to ramble for an hour, drinking in the sights and sounds of the city. Then, glancing at his watch, he hailed a cab and gave the address of one of the more discreet restaurants in the city that catered to the gay set.

He ate alone although he was aware that he attracted a certain amount of attention. The mere arrival of a stranger in these places was always of some interest, particularly a nice-looking one whose clothes and demeanor suggested money and breeding. To his disappointment, however, there was no direct attempt to establish contact.

He left the restaurant and went on to the next place on his list, a rather smart lounge with soft lighting and deep carpet on the floor. The evening crowds were already beginning to gather. Hopefully he would do better here. Although neither of them gave any sign of recognition to one another, the bartender was an agent of C.A.M.P., primarily working to provide information. By now he would have let discreet hints drop to the regular patrons about Jackie's visit.

He seemed doomed to disappointment here, as well. He was cruised several times, but nothing appeared to be of any real significance. Jackie started a second drink and was on the verge of deciding to move on to the next bar when a familiar voice greeted him from over his shoulder.

"Well, I see you're out looking for a little fun," Bruce said.

Jackie turned around, pleased to be remembered. "Looking," he agreed. "But not succeeding."

"Well, no wonder, you pick the stuffiest places," Bruce kidded him. "I rarely come here myself. It's usually dull."

"What brings you here tonight?" Jackie asked, genuinely pleased. If the rest of the evening proved as unsuccessful as the first part of it had done, he might do well to work on the blond after all.

Bruce shrugged and gave him a coy grin. "Maybe it's Fate," he suggested. "Come on, why don't you let me give you the tour? I can show you some of the really fun places."

Jackie hesitated. His rule was always business before pleasure, but so far he hadn't managed to do any business. And, he reminded himself, he might do even better in the "fun" places."

"You've got yourself an escort," he said, polishing off his drink. "But only if I can pick up the tab."

"Don't be silly," Bruce said, but Jackie was adamant.

"I insist," he said. He produced a twenty with a flourish that was not wasted on the others around them and put it on the bar. "For my drink," he told the bartender. "And keep the change."

* * * * * * *

The evening went by quickly in a profusion of bars, drinks and music. Bruce proved a knowledgeable and charming guide and if Jackie seemed to be making no progress he was at least making his presence in the city known, and having a ball while he was at it.

Bruce introduced him to friends in each bar and Jackie made a point of flashing money, buying rounds of drinks for everyone and other such ruses.

"You've got yourself a real find there," one of Bruce's friends, a rather rough-looking piece of trade, commented at one point. "Better hang on to him."

Although he pretended not to hear the remark, Jackie wondered if the friend, a ruthlessly handsome young man named Fred, might not be the contact he was seeking. He did not, however, have an opportunity to play up to Fred, as a few minutes later Bruce was ready to move on.

"Getting tired yet?" Bruce asked when they were outside on the sidewalk.

"Just getting warmed up," Jackie insisted. "Where to next?"

Bruce rolled his eyes thoughtfully for a minute. "How about dancing our cares away?" he suggested.

"Sounds great," Jackie agreed eagerly, "Know anyplace where we can?" Even in a city as liberal as San Francisco, it was still illegal for two men to dance together. There were inevitably clubs where that happened, but they were secretive and known only to insiders.

"Coming right up," Bruce answered. "It's just around the corner; we can walk to this one."

Jackie wondered, as they approached the spot, if Bruce was maybe pulling his leg. There was no evidence of any sort of a bar, only a neighborhood theater that was already closed for the evening. Next door to it a flight of steep stairs went up to what, according to the sign outside, was a health club.

"This is the place," Bruce informed him, indicating the stairs.

"I thought you said dancing," Jackie said, although he followed Bruce upward. "If you want to wrestle why not go to my hotel?"

"You'll see," Bruce said back over his shoulder with a grin.

From the moment they entered the door upstairs it was obvious that Bruce had made no mistake. The health club sign was only a fake, for this was a gay bar and a rather lively one. They entered first into a crowded room filled with small tables and a bar where customers crowded together. Beyond that room were more tables grouped around a vast dance floor that was filled with young men dancing together.

"I'll be damned," Jackie said, staring about in amazement as they took a table. This was a new one on him and he had thought he knew the city well.

"It's new," Bruce explained when they had ordered drinks. "Only been here a few weeks. Would you like to dance?"

Jackie felt a pang of guilt. The music blaring over the speakers was the latest hit record of Dingo Stark. Remembering Stark, he could not help feeling depressed that he had made no more progress than he had. But he was here and it would not do to let his facade slip.

"Sure, I'd love to," he said, forcing a smile to his lips again.

They moved together to the already crowded dance floor. Bruce began to move at once, twisting and writhing in time to the music.

"Do you do the Dog?" he asked Jackie.

"Of course," Jackie assured him, and began to perform the dance in question. The Dog, in his opinion, was rather close to simulating the real thing. It had been banned, he knew, in many of the more conservative discotheques, particularly those catering to the teenage crowds. Its blatant gestures and movements, however, were those with which Jackie was quite familiar. His hips jerked back and forth in time to the heavy beat of Dingo's song. Bruce bent and crouched and leaning over him Jackie went through all the same motions he would have used in bed. To a bystander, even one a few feet away, it could only have looked as though the two were making love.

"Hey, you're a great dancer," Bruce said admiringly.

"I studied under Villanova," Jackie told him without conceit. He did not add that a shelf in his apartment displayed numerous dancing trophies he had won. There was virtually no dance that he had not mastered. He had once stepped in, unannounced, for the lead dancer in Swan Lake. It wasn't only classical ballet, however, that he had mastered. He could do all the popular dances as well, from the Watusi to the Frog—and the Dog.

The record ended and they returned to their table where their drinks were waiting for them. "You know," Bruce said, pulling his chair close, "when I met you on the plane, I figured you for the very dull type. But you're great fun."

"I can be even more entertaining," Jackie told him suggestively. He took advantage of the dim lights to lay one hand on Bruce's thick leg. There was no protest and he got a little bolder, inching his fingers upward. He reached the warm area of the thighs, tingling with excitement as his fingers crept up and up, finally finding their goal. Bruce was big and Jackie's hand rubbed affectionately creating a familiar response.

"Hey, I won't be able to walk out of here," Bruce warned him. "Better wait until later."

"I'm ready for you now," Jackie told him hoarsely. It was nearly time for the bars to be closing so he would not be wasting his working hours by indulging in a little fun. "My hotel isn't far."

Bruce shook his head. "Hotels can be risky," he said. "What's wrong with my place?"

"Not a thing," Jackie said. He left a ten on the table to pay for the drinks and a minute later they were on their way out of the bar, Bruce walking rather stiffly and holding his hand in front of his trousers to conceal the results of Jackie's efforts.

♠ CHAPTER SIX ♠
λ

Bruce's apartment was not far. If Jackie had retained any doubts about Bruce's sincerity they had been dispelled by Bruce's remarks about the hotel. He was obviously being thoughtful in pointing out the risk of going back to the hotel and that was an unlikely gesture from a blackmailer.

The apartment was small, and rather plain, bearing the recognizable stamp of a place that was rented furnished. "It's not much," Bruce said as they entered. "But I'm only using it temporarily."

"And then?" Jackie prompted.

Bruce shrugged. "Who knows? I'm not the sort to be tied down for long."

A man after my own heart, Jackie decided, but left the statement unsaid.

"Want a drink?" Bruce asked, pausing in the middle of the room.

"I don't need it," Jackie assured him, stepping closer. He was eager for another try at the exciting flesh he had fondled earlier.

"You know," Bruce said when the kiss had ended, "I didn't think you'd be the amorous type either."

"Still waters run deep," Jackie reminded him, nibbling at one pink ear. The zipper of Bruce's trousers was no match for his experienced fingers. And he felt even better without all that cloth in the way.

"Okay, you win," Bruce said with a low chuckle. "The bedroom's this way."

In the bedroom Jackie did not wait for the disrobing process. He kissed Bruce again, hungrily. "I want you," he whispered, stroking and fondling his companion to increased excitement.

Bruce smiled and slid from the embrace, dropping across the bed. Jackie joined him, fumbling with the trousers again. Bruce raised his hips in response to the tugging hands and Jackie pulled the trousers down over his hips to below his knees. His eyes feasted on the harvest of loveliness framed by the blue of the bedspread.

"Beautiful," he whispered without exaggeration. It was like a scene from a Renaissance painting: the delicate pink-and-white skin, full-blown loveliness, the graceful curve of the hips. He lowered his face, kissing the yielding softness of the stomach, his mouth finding its way lower. Bruce trembled as the eager lips reached their goal, the darting tongue sending ripples of excitement through him. Jackie's kisses were everywhere, teasing, exciting, urging, until the blond young man was panting with lust, his body ripe for taking.

With the help of Bruce's trembling hands Jackie shed his own clothes, not taking the time to remove such trivialities as T-shirt and socks. His slacks and shorts about his ankles, he fell backward over the bed as Bruce returned the homage Jackie had paid his body.

He was good, Jackie discovered, quite good, and wonderful to be with. With all of the dancing and running about he still had a scent of cleanliness and soap, as though he had just emerged from a shower. His skin, like pink velvet, was a delight to stroke and fondle. Gentle wisps of blond hair fell across Jackie's naked thighs. With a moan of pleasure Jackie turned, locking their bodies together. He devoured the quivering body hungrily.

In unison they lunged and thrust, their tempo racing madly as they abandoned themselves to their orgy of lust. Jackie's hands clung to the tender softness of the full cheeks, pinning Bruce to him until he felt the final swelling and then the shuddering paroxysm of release. Seconds later he too yielded up the fruits of his passion in a long, shattering peak.

Limp and breathless, they fell apart, lying in silence as they savored the lingering sweetness. "Still think I'm not the amorous type?" Jackie asked finally, reaching out to stroke the naked body with affection.

"Like a mink," Bruce said with a sigh.

Jackie pulled himself to a sitting position and began to rearrange his clothes. "It's late, he said. "I'd better be getting back to my hotel."

"Stick around," Bruce suggested, grabbing him playfully. "It only takes me a minute or two to get my breath again."

"You mean you're one of those all-night-long types?" Jackie asked, continuing with his clothes anyway.

"It's always better the second time," Bruce said with a pout.

And besides, Jackie thought, your friend might not have gotten all the pictures he needed. He had not overlooked the slightly open door to the closet nor had his ears missed the click of the camera. He understood now the reason for suggesting this place instead of the hotel. At the hotel they would have been alone. Here, Bruce's friend, whoever was in the closet, was waiting with a camera. It had been a successful evening after all, in every way. Now all he had to do was wait for them to make the next move.

Bruce seemed to give up his persuasion and in fact grew somewhat thoughtful as he waited for Jackie to dress. "I'll see you to the door," he said finally, pulling up his own trousers.

"It's not necessary," Jackie assured him.

"But nice," Bruce insisted. At the door they kissed, a long, torrid embrace that almost made Jackie change his mind about staying.

"You know," Bruce said, looking into Jackie's eyes with a peculiar sadness. "I like you."

"I should hope," Jackie answered with a grin. "You wouldn't do this sort of thing with people you didn't like, would you?" He made it sound like an innocent jest, but the remark struck home. Bruce scowled and almost said something before he caught himself.

"Of course not," he said, returning the grin with one of his own that would not have fooled anyone.

Outside, Jackie started off down the street. He walked until he was sure he was out of sight from the apartment building before sprinting across the street and doubling back, staying to the shadows. When he was across the street from Bruce's apartment he took up a post where he would not be seen and waited.

He did not have long to wait. Ten minutes later Fred, the rough trade type he had met earlier, emerged from the building, a camera case over his arm.

So that was it. Bruce had used the guided tour as an excuse to put him on display and get Fred's approval or disapproval. Some sort of signal had been given, telling Bruce to proceed, and the rest had been easy.

Fred climbed into a Jaguar XKE parked at the curb and a minute later roared away. Jackie waited until the taillights were out of sight before stepping to the sidewalk and starting off again for the hotel. He smiled to himself as he walked, thinking of the blond he had held in his arms a short while before.

Not a bad way, he decided to work on a case.

* * * * * * *

He did not have long to wait. The first thing Jackie saw when he awoke in his hotel room the following morning was the envelope that had been pushed under the door.

They were crude pictures, badly lighted and hastily developed, but they were sufficient for their purpose. He was easily recognizable in all of them and so were the activities in which he was engaged. None of them that had been sent, however, showed Bruce's face. No doubt they had destroyed any from which he could be identified—or maybe they kept them as a weapon against Bruce, insurance that he would never defect.

Studying Bruce's body as it was in the pictures and remembering it as it had been in his arms, Jackie felt a moment of sadness. He had actually liked the blond and had genuinely enjoyed their evening together. It was sad that the evil fingers of B.U.T.C.H. should be able to taint so many lives. How many other young men would be brought into their web unless he could somehow destroy the organization, strike at its very roots?

There was a note with the pictures. It was brief and to the point. He was to deliver one hundred thousand dollars in cash, that same night. The money was to be in a paper bag. He would leave it in a trashcan just outside some certain public restrooms at Golden Gate Park.

Things were beginning to break at last. He had made contact with the ring of blackmailers. The rest he would have to play by instinct. One thing was certain, however, he would keep the appointment, with the money. Capturing them in the park would accomplish nothing. He would only be capturing one or two of the smaller people and the ring would still be in operation, free to do more harm to other innocent people. He had to let them lead him to their home base so that his blow, when he struck, would be a fatal one.

He went to the phone and placed a call to Los Angeles, to one of the numerous telephone numbers utilized by C.A.M.P. It would be simpler to contact the local office directly, but risky. He was supposed to be a stranger in town who knew no one and if his activities were being watched he did not want to make anyone suspicious of him. It was essential that they continue to think of him as a helpless victim.

Rich's voice was a welcome sound. It was a source of comfort to know that whatever he needed would be attended to quickly and efficiently.

"It's Jackie Garden," he identified himself, using the phony name. "Remember me?"

"How could I forget?" Rich answered in a voice that was deceptively polite and unfamiliar, as near strangers would be with one another.

"I only wanted to thank you for a lovely evening while in Los Angeles. I hope I'll see you again when I get into town. I may be stopping back that way in a few days."

"Aren't things going well for you in San Francisco?" Rich asked. "It's really quite a lovely city."

"Oh, I've found it quite exciting," Jackie answered. "I've met some fascinating people and I have a number of things to do the next day or so." The statement, innocent enough, would let Rich know that things were happening as he had hoped.

"Well, let me know if there's anything I can do for you. I have a few friends there, you know."

"As a matter of fact there is something." Jackie kept his tone conversational as he got around to his real reason for calling. "I had a slight accident with one of my jackets. I wonder if you can recommend a tailor who can repair it for me?"

"I know a fine one," Rich assured him. "Why don't I send you to him?"

"That might be difficult. I can't very well go out with my jacket torn you know, and I wanted to wear it tonight, so it is a bit urgent. Do you suppose you could send him around to the hotel?"

"No problem," Rich assured him. "He's an old friend of mine. I'll see that he's there in no time."

Jackie hung up the phone, satisfied. He ordered breakfast sent up to his room and waited confidently for Rich's "tailor" to arrive.

The man was there within the hour. Jackie recognized him at once as an agent with whom he had worked before, although the gray-haired, withered figure looked like anything but an agent from C.A.M.P.

"My dear," the man greeted him when they were alone in the room, "Why didn't you let me know you were in town? Is this a vacation, or are you working on something?"

"Working," Jackie assured him. "And in need of a little assistance."

"Well, pour your mother a cup of coffee," his guest said, discarding his pose of a helpless old man and behaving like the flaming queen he was, "and tell me what I can do for you."

Jackie explained as he poured the coffee from the pot that had been supplied by room service. "First thing, I'll need some cash, a hundred thousand dollars, to be specific."

The gray eyebrows shot up. "Heavens, extravagant little thing, aren't you?"

"Charge it to our office, Rich will clear it. And I want a homing device planted in the money. I'll leave that up to you how you hide it. Then I'll need a car, one that will pick up the signals."

"Anything else?"

Jackie considered the matter for a moment. He could be walking into a lion's den. It would be comforting to know that someone else was on hand to help out if the going got too rough. That could mean scaring off his enemies, however.

"I guess that's it," he answered finally. "Can you get them to me here by this afternoon?"

"The garage man is an old friend. I'll talk to him. You call down this afternoon and say you'd like to rent a car. He'll see you get the right one." He finished his coffee and left a few minutes later.

Jackie waited until the man had ample time to leave the building before he called room service to remove his tray. Then he dressed and went out himself. There was nothing more to be done until afternoon and he might as well take advantage of the opportunity to see a little more of the city.

He paused in the lobby, near a counter where fresh flowers were on display. With a grin he approached the woman there and ordered two dozen roses sent to Bruce at his apartment. He wrote the note himself, thanking Bruce for a lovely evening and expressing his wish that they might get together again. He sealed the note, leaving it to be sent with the flowers, and left the hotel whistling.

THE MAN FROM C.A.M.P.

♠ CHAPTER SEVEN ♠
λ

He enjoyed a harmless bout of sightseeing and returned to the hotel shortly after lunch. He was surprised and puzzled to find a message for him, asking him to call a Mr. Benton at another hotel. The name meant nothing to him, and aside from Bruce or someone from C.A.M.P., he could not imagine what reason anyone in the city would have for calling him.

He waited until he was in his room before placing the call. There was a brief delay while the other switchboard rang the correct room and then a familiar voice answered.

"Dingo," he said, amazed.

"Jackie?" It was indeed Dingo Stark's voice on the other end of the line.

"What the hell are you doing in town?"

"I had my manager arrange it so I could see you," Dingo explained, speaking quickly. "I've got quite a bit to tell you. Can you come by over here for a visit soon?"

"I'll be there in fifteen minutes," Jackie said. He hung up the phone and was on his way at once. Dingo had not sounded very happy over the phone and it would have to be something important that had made the singer risk coming here, to San Francisco.

Dingo greeted him at the door, his expression a mixed one of relief to see Jackie, and obvious concern,

"What's up?" Jackie asked, coming into the hotel room.

"Several things," Dingo said quickly. "In the first place I thought you'd want to know I found Steve. Jackie Holmes, this is Steve Simon."

Jackie stopped as the young man rose from the chair in which he was seated and stepped forward, his hand extended. Dingo had described Steve properly as delicate and fragile. His blue-black hair, neatly combed in contrast to Dingo's unruly tresses, framed the sort of face that had once belonged to china dolls. His flawless skin was the color of fresh milk. Large dark eyes peered out at him beneath long, lustrous lashes. His nose was a brief, curt exclamation mark over a small, pouting mouth. Slender of body, he stood no more than five six. It was little wonder, Jackie thought quickly, that Steve had aroused the protective instincts in Dingo, and that Dingo had found himself drawn more and more to the pretty, innocently helpless creature.

"The pleasure," Jackie said aloud, "is all mine, I assure you."

"I found him in Los Angeles," Dingo explained. His tone seemed unusually curt, and Jackie wondered if Dingo weren't still quite attached to the

74

young man and perhaps a little jealous of the warm smile Steve was showering upon him now. "He'd moved back from San Francisco. I thought you'd want to meet him, so I persuaded him to come up here with me."

"Dingo's told me about his trouble," Steve said in a soft, musical voice. "And we're both grateful for all you're doing to help him."

Jackie thought of how grateful Dingo could be and wondered briefly if Steve would be willing to offer the same reward. With such a double incentive he could probably clean up the case in half the time.

"It looks like things are going our way," he said aloud. "At least I've got a lead."

"I hope it moves fast," Dingo said grimly. "I've been contacted again."

"About the diaries?" B.U.T.C.H. had the diaries now and they would certainly use them as an added tool to pry money out of Dingo.

Dingo nodded and handed him a brown envelope. Jackie opened it and pulled out the contents. There were only two sheets of paper and a note. The note was brief and to the point:

> *"Would you like to see this book circulating all over the world? If not, come up with $300,000. We'll contact you again in five days and tell you where to leave it."*

The sheets of paper were Xeroxed copies of two pages from the diary. Jackie glanced at the first. It was a description, in Dingo's own narrative, of a

75

sexual incident between him and Steve. Jackie read only the first two lines and then out of courtesy returned the sheets to the envelope.

"$300,000? They raised their prices," he commented, handing the envelope back to Dingo.

"They've got good reason," Dingo reminded him. "From my standpoint these are pretty valuable papers. They're worth a lot more than mere stories whispered about."

"At least they've given us some time," Jackie said. "We've go a week to beat them to the punch."

"Will it be long enough?" Steve asked in his low voice.

"If our luck holds out, yes. I've already made contact and should meet some of our friends tonight."

"Do you think you can get the diaries that soon?" Steve asked anxiously.

Jackie sensed that the affection between the two had not been only one way. Steve's concern was obvious.

"Nothing's really certain," he warned them. "But I'm certainly going to try. Will you two be in town?"

"We can stay for a few days," Dingo answered. "My agent canceled a few appointments for me. I was too upset about all this to keep my mind on business anyway."

"Stay in this same hotel," Jackie told them, preparing to leave. "I'll be in touch as soon as I have anything to report."

The image of Steve's pretty, concerned face stayed with Jackie as he left the room and started back for his own hotel.

* * * * * * *

A short while before he was to keep his appointment, Jackie phoned to the desk of his hotel and inquired about renting a car. He was assured that a car would be ready for him whenever he wished. Jackie asked that it brought around to the front.

Before leaving his room he unlocked his briefcase and set it atop the bed. Carefully removing the innocent papers inside, he flicked a concealed latch and the inside lining fell away to reveal a hidden compartment. Jackie removed a gun from the space, a small, stunningly-jeweled Derringer. It was not a particularly potent weapon. The gun fired only one shot, and was of such a small caliber that it was ineffective beyond a close range. It was the one he preferred to use, however, as an emergency weapon. As an agent for C.A.M.P., he had no authority to kill and the gun was solely for protection when necessary. He relied far more upon his wits and his physical abilities.

He fitted the gun neatly into a small holster under his jacket. The slight bulge it produced was scarcely noticeable. Giving the weapon a pat, Jackie let himself out of his room and started for the lobby.

A new yellow Plymouth was pulling up to the front entrance as he went out the door. The driver leaned out of the window. "Mr. Garden?" he asked anxiously.

"That's me," Jackie said. The garage-man had a right to be worried. Giving a car with a built-in homing device and a bag full of money to the wrong person could be a big mistake.

The driver gave a quick sigh of relief and scooted out of the car, turning it over to Jackie. Out of the corner of his eye, Jackie noted the paper bag on the floor. Everything was ready for him as he had instructed. On the dash a pale green light displayed the signal from the homing device hidden in the money. He tipped the driver handsomely and drove away.

* * * * * * *

Golden Gate Park was a vast area of neatly preserved beauty. There were acres of grounds that included duck ponds, rustic woods and even a Japanese Tea Garden, a spot Jackie had often visited in the past to enjoy the quiet loveliness. In addition, there were countless exhibit buildings, even a reptile display and a band shell for outdoor concerts.

Today, however, he was not here to enjoy San Francisco's famed park. It was already evening, the shadows long and ominous over the ground. The crowds of people who had explored the park during the day were now on their way home or back to their hotels. Long lines waited at the bus stops and a crush of automobile traffic moved slowly down the park's drives.

Jackie left his car as near as possible to the restrooms that had been selected for depositing the money. He took the sack with him under his arm and walked across the lawn toward the building. The wastebasket outside was already filled with the day's debris and he wondered briefly about the possibility of some conscientious custodian emptying the containers before the money was collected. But no doubt B.U.T.C.H, always efficient, had thought of that and taken the necessary precautions.

He paused as a solitary figure came out of the restroom, giving him a questioning glance. Jackie ignored the pointed look. Another time he might have cruised a bit but on this occasion he had more important things to attend to.

He waited until the stranger, discouraged by the lack of response, had started away, his back to Jackie. There was no one else close by and Jackie dropped the paper bag containing the money into the waste can as he entered the restroom, accomplishing the trick in one quick, almost imperceptible movement.

Inside the building he attended to his bodily functions without haste, in order not to make himself look suspicious. Then, without even glancing in the direction of the waste can, he left and strolled leisurely back to his car.

It was dark by now and the park nearly empty. From time to time a solitary figure could be seen strolling about, usually watching for some other lonely figure with whom to share a few minutes. Like all big-city parks, Golden Gate Park attracted the lonely gays.

In the distance Jackie saw a pitiful looking tramp wandering slowly along, his pace labored, his shoulders stooped. He felt a pang of sympathy. There were so many unfortunates in the world. If only he could help them all. But he had chosen a cause and dedicated himself to it. His strength and

his resources must be devoted solely to that one
cause if he was to be effective.

As he watched, the bedraggled creature
changed his course of direction and started toward
the restrooms. To Jackie's alarm he paused at the
wastebasket and began to rummage through its contents. The man was certain to find the sack full of
money and his plans, as well as those of
B.U.T.C.H., would be thwarted. He opened the door
of his car and put one foot to the ground.

No, he realized suddenly, this was not some
chance mishap that Fate had thrown in their paths.
The tramp appeared to be rummaging merely for
something to eat but even as he pawed through the
refuse he had already removed the bag containing
the money and set it carefully aside. After a moment
he started away, the money tucked neatly under his
arm.

Jackie smiled to himself and closed his car
door again. Very neat, in case anyone was watching.
The man had moved off down one of the many
paths that passed through the park. Mentally Jackie
reviewed the layout of the park, which he had committed to memory, judging where the man's route
would take him. Then, starting up the engine of the
Plymouth, he drove slowly forward, taking the ve-
hicular route that would carry him to the same destination.

There was another car ahead of him. Jackie
moved slowly behind it, keeping it within sight as
he came down another drive in time to see the tramp
emerge from the trees in the distance. The door of
the waiting car opened, the money was handed in-

side and the car pulled quickly away as the tramp ambled across the road at a leisurely pace.

All very slick, Jackie thought. He drove carefully, dropping behind and out of sight. With the homing device buried in the money carefully giving him directions, it was not necessary that he keep within sight of the car he was following. Wherever they went he would follow. With luck they would lead him to their home base, the very heart of B.U.T.C.H.

That was something he had long searched for and the prospect of success at last filled him with tingling excitement. This could prove far more important than Dingo Stark's diaries. It could mean safety for hundreds and thousands of homosexuals.

THE MAN FROM C.A.M.P.

♠ CHAPTER EIGHT ♠
λ

The route that they were following carried them back downtown. Jackie drove with one eye on the evening traffic and the other on the dashboard, watching the signal that was giving him directions. The brilliance of downtown San Francisco by night spread around him. Market Street was a bawdy river of sailors in tight-fitting uniforms and high-voiced, effeminate young men. Cheap arcades and magazine shops, that he knew displayed blatantly erotic pictures and books, lined the sidewalks. Theaters advertised vulgar girlie movies. It was an area that reeked of vice, sex and unconcealed desire.

They turned and left behind the tawdry atmosphere of Market Street. He realized they were heading toward Chinatown—a city within a city, another world almost. His heart beat faster as he sensed that they were near their destination.

The signal from the dashboard told him that the car ahead had stopped. Jackie drove slowly, dodging the streams of cars and pedestrians. Here the tourists were out in full force, for Chinatown was a sight to be seen by night as well as by day. Strange, exotic buildings were silhouetted against the San Francisco sky. Quaint shops offered works of art and tourist junk together and dimly lighted side streets and alleys hinted at adventure and danger.

He saw the car he had been following parked at the curb ahead of him. He drove by it, seeking a parking place of his own and found it on the next block. He parked and walked back, blending in with the crowds of tourist, moving inconspicuously.

The car was still where he had seen it. Jackie paused as he approached, glancing about. Just past the spot a narrow alleyway led from the busy street. Jackie glanced at it as though he were merely a curious visitor and then stepped into it, starting down its dim path.

It was a singular experience, as though a curtain had been closed upon the activity and rush of the city. Here, with only a few steps, he had left behind the tourist attractions and the gaudy displays. All was quiet. The signs displayed no English and the unfamiliar Chinese symbols on a few of the doors made them appear all the more mysterious and ominous.

There was no way of knowing into which door his adversaries had disappeared. Nothing stirred except a big, indolent cat that glowered at him for a minute before disappearing into a shadow.

Still another passageway opened off this one, a few feet of narrow tunnel that dropped down a short, steep flight of steps to a basement type building. The shades had been drawn over the door and window but beyond that a dim light could be seen.

As he listened he heard the muffled sound of voices that seemed to be arguing.

He hesitated for a moment and then started down. It could be something perfectly innocent, unrelated to his search—perhaps a family discussion or an argument over prices. The risk would have to be taken, however. He was convinced his quarry was somewhere in this alley, behind one of the closed doors. If necessary he would find some way to search the entire area, until he had caught the rats in their nest.

His foot struck a stone on one of the steps and sent it clattering down before him. Ahead, the voices beyond the door grew silent. Jackie froze where he was. His presence had been clumsily announced. Would he find himself facing some irate resident? Or something more dangerous?

The silence continued. As he stood motionless, Jackie hit upon a scheme that might save him some embarrassment. He would ask directions to some special shop that had been recommended to him. That would give him the opportunity to see who was inside and also explain his presence if this were not the right door.

He started down again and reached the door. Without pause he knocked loudly. A minute later the door opened on a wizened, yellow-faced figure who would have looked more appropriate clad in the traditional garments of his past than in the typically Western suit he was wearing.

"I'm trying to find the shop of Lin Chan," Jackie answered the unspoken question in the man's eyes. "I seem to be having some trouble locating it."

The man screwed up his face. "I do not know that shop," he said in a cracked voice. "But come in, please. I will ask my daughter if she can direct you."

Jackie felt a warning tickle at his scalp but there was no logical way to retreat now. Tense beneath the deceptively innocent air he feigned, he followed the old man inside.

He had no sooner stepped over the threshold than the door was closed swiftly behind him. Jackie whirled about to find himself facing the same threesome he had met before, the ones who had attacked Dingo Stark. Bruno Scotto's evil face leered at him malevolently.

"I'm afraid, Mr. Garden," the Oriental man was saying, "that you've been impetuous."

Jackie had no time to answer. He reached instinctively for the gun under his jacket but the three thugs were faster. Scotto was upon him in a rush, his massive fist connecting with Jackie's jaw before Jackie had time to dodge the blow. Someone grabbed him from behind. Jackie grabbed and twisted, lifting the man up and using his hip as a lever to fling his assailant into the air and against Bruno Scotto.

There was no time, however, to protect himself from the gun barrel that crashed against the back of his head. He pitched silently forward, unconscious.

* * * * * *

Jackie awoke in darkness, the floor damp and cold beneath him. He stirred, half surprised to find himself alive and functioning. Finally, expecting another blow at any minute, he lifted his head and looked around.

He was in the same place, he decided as his eyes became accustomed to the darkness. And he was alone. The door had been left open, evidence of the fact that his assailants had made a hasty departure.

He rose, rubbing his head gently. This was getting to be a habit and a dangerous one. Apparently Bruno and the others hadn't recognized him except as Jackie Garden, and for that reason hadn't considered him important enough or dangerous enough to kill. But they had made their escape.

He flicked on the light and looked around the single room. It had been stripped, leaving nothing behind in the way of clues. Only the paper bag that had once contained the money was lying crumpled on the floor. Jackie stooped and picked it up. Hidden in one of the seams at the bottom of the bag was the homing device that had allowed him to follow them before. Obviously they had transferred the money to some other container and cheated him of a trail to follow.

He had lost his prey and a sizable bundle of cash as well. Things weren't going so nicely after all. With a grimace, he left the room and retraced his steps back to the street. He had only been unconscious a short time and Chinatown was still active. Discouraged, Jackie found his car and drove back to his hotel.

There was a message at the desk that Steve Simon had called. Jackie crumpled up the paper as he made his way to the elevator. He hadn't the heart to call and tell Dingo and Steve how badly things had gone this evening. In the morning would be soon enough.

The elevator operator, a rather homely young man whom Jackie suspected of knowing the score, gave him a conspiratorial wink as they rode up. "I let your brother into your room," he said in a low voice.

"My brother?" Jackie repeated, puzzled.

"Well, that's what he called himself," the operator told him with a knowing grin. "Don't worry, I fixed it with one of the maids. No one else knows about it except us."

Jackie nodded his head. "I see." He removed his billfold and took out two five dollar bills, slipping them into the ready hand. "Thanks for your trouble and tell the maid the same."

In the hall upstairs he paused and felt under his jacket. The Derringer was still there, undiscovered by the thugs he had tangled with earlier. He drew it and advanced stealthily toward his room.

There was no way of unlocking the door noiselessly. The key grated loudly in the lock. Holding his breath, Jackie moved to one side and kicked the door open with his foot. Nothing happened. With a quick movement, he stepped into the opening.

Bruce Hamilton smiled at him from the bed. "Don't you think you'd better come in and close that door," he said, "Before someone comes by and sees me?"

It was a good suggestion. The attractive blond had made himself at home. The bedclothes were turned down and Bruce was stark naked upon the white surface of the sheet. The soft light from the lamp played seductively upon his pale skin.

Jackie came into the room and closed the door after himself. "Very cute," he said sarcastically, the gun still drawn. "Let's have an explanation and make it fast."

Bruce rolled his eyes innocently. "I told you the other night I liked you."

Jackie moved across the room warily. "You mean you need some more pictures for your collection?" he sneered. He opened the closet door but it was empty except for his clothes.

"If you're looking for Fred," Bruce said, "he isn't here. I'm alone, doll."

Jackie glowered at the naked young man, trying not to let his eyes be dazzled by the pink-white flesh that was all the more inviting as he began remembering the feel of it against his own.

"Okay," he said, returning the gun to its holster. "Let's have it. Why the hell are you here, like that?"

"If you mean naked when you say like that, I thought it was a lovely idea. Saves a lot of time undressing after you arrive."

"What makes you think I'd have asked you to undress," Jackie demanded, although he knew full well his voice wasn't very convincing. "And what brought you here in the first place? Did your friends cut you out on the pay off?"

"Did you pay?" Bruce asked.

"I didn't have much choice."

"You know, it's peculiar, but I wouldn't have thought the other night that you were the sort to carry a gun."

"I have to, playing around with your kind of friends. Did they send you?"

"They'd kill me if they found out I was here," Bruce said, sounding as though he meant it. "Will you believe me if I say I'm sorry?"

Jackie sighed and forced himself to look the other way. "It's a little late for that, isn't it?

"I guess it is," Bruce said, discarding his flippant tone. "But you see, I had no choice. They have a very extensive collection of pictures of me, to say nothing of a few other items that cause a lot of trouble for me. I have to do what they tell me to do, even if I don't like it."

It was a typical B.U.T.C.H. tactic, Jackie knew. He relented slightly, although he couldn't help feeling a little angry.

"Okay," he said, "You've made your apologies. Now you'd better put on your clothes and beat it so I can get some rest."

"You don't really want me to go," Bruce said.

Jackie looked back, wetting his lips with his tongue. Bruce's hands were busy making himself all the more conspicuous—and desirable.

"Stop that," he growled. His own trousers were beginning to feel uncomfortably tight as he watched.

"I will," Bruce told him with a knowing smile. "If you do it for me."

Jackie weakened. Even if he had been duped the last time, he had gotten his money's worth sexually. And here it was being offered to him again, for free this time. He stepped closer, standing by the edge of the bed to stare down at the inviting expanse of male beauty.

Bruce pulled himself up on his elbows. One hand reached for the zipper of Jackie's trousers and Jackie's leg trembled slightly as the searching hand found him. It was a winning argument. He unfastened his belt and allowed Bruce to pull his trousers downward. Together they got them off. The rest of his clothes were not far behind.

Bruce's thick thighs parted as Jackie lowered himself to the bed, his own flesh as solid and as ready as Bruce's.

"I want you there," Bruce whispered, guiding him with his hand. Jackie was only too happy to comply. He thrust his hips forward and felt the yielding softness of warm flesh. Bruce groaned, his legs lifted high, his body bent almost double.

Jackie didn't try to be kind. He was venting what was left of his anger on the tender, fleshy bottom turned up to him, his thrashing hips moving with speed and violence.

Not that Bruce regarded it as punishment. He squirmed and moaned deliriously, arching his back to raise himself, meeting each energetic push.

Jackie bent, his hands clasping Bruce's wriggling hips and lifting until his eager lips reached Bruce's towering flesh.

It was a whirlwind of motion and sensation as they struggled together, their bodies' white hot with passion and surging lust.

Jackie felt the warning stirring within himself as their ardor approached its zenith. He strained to control himself until Bruce's breathing had become a succession of labored gasps, his flesh swelling and trembling in a telltale manner. Then, together, they exploded in a flood of searing pleasure.

THE MAN FROM C.A.M.P.

♠ CHAPTER NINE ♠
λ

It seemed an eternity later that they finally stirred and separated. Jackie sat up and lighted a cigarette.

"All right," he said. "Now suppose you tell me what all that was about?"

Bruce grinned and sat up as well, snuggling close against Jackie's nude body. "I wanted to see if it would be as great a second time with you as it was the first."

That was an answer Jackie could understand. He knew without conceit that he was good in bed. Sex was, after all, his favorite pastime as well as an essential tool in his arsenal of weapons and he had devoted himself to mastering the subject.

"Still sore at me?" Bruce asked finally in a sober tone.

"No, I guess not." Jackie said, rubbing one hand affectionately over the soft buttocks. "I believe what you said about not having any choice in the matter."

"I can make it up to you," Bruce said, raising himself on one elbow. "I could get the pictures back. I was hoping maybe I could get to you before you paid them."

"Isn't that dangerous?" Jackie asked, his interest aroused.

"Not if they don't find out who took them," Bruce explained. "If I'm careful no one will be wiser. But of course it's too late to worry about the pictures now, since you've already paid them."

"There's something else more important than those pictures." Jackie said thinking of Dingo Stark and the diary. "Something I want to get badly. Can you show me where they are kept?"

Bruce frowned and shook his head. "That would be dangerous. If anyone saw you there they'd suspect me at once. But I could get it for you if you let me know what it is."

"It's a diary," Jackie explained. It was a gamble he knew, but he had to trust someone and Bruce was his only link now with the ring. He described the notebook to the silent blond.

"Are you a cop?" Bruce asked finally.

"Of sorts," Jackie admitted. "I'm an agent for C.A.M.P."

Bruce's eyebrows went up. "So that's it. No wonder you had the gun and all. Hell, I would get killed if they knew about this."

Jackie frowned. "You're right about that. It's dangerous for you to be helping me.

Bruce gave him a smile as he stood and began to dress himself. "I can be pretty cagey myself, you know. I'll get the diary for you. I owe you that much at least."

"How will you get it to me?" Jackie asked.

"You'll have to pick it up at my place," Bruce said. "Don't worry. They rarely come around there unless it's to take pictures. There's a back stairs to the building. Come in that way. It's safe. I'll have a *Do Not Disturb* sign tacked to the door."

Bruce, dressed again for the street, came back to the bed and bent down to kiss him. "Of course," he said softly. "I'll expect a reward. A repeat performance."

"You'll get it," Jackie assured him and meant it. "Tomorrow night?"

"Make it afternoon," Bruce said. "I'll have the book by then. Come around at two o'clock."

Jackie sat for a long time in the bed after Bruce had left, contemplating this turn of events. At least if things went well he would have Dingo's diary back. And, if he played it right, he might yet persuade Bruce to lead him to the B.U.T.C.H. headquarters. By this time he owed those hoods, especially Bruno Scotto, quite a few lumps on the head. And that was one debt he was eager to pay off.

* * * * * * *

First thing when he awoke in the morning, which was not until almost noon, Jackie called Dingo at his hotel. It was not the singer, but Steve who answered the phone.

"Jackie," Steve greeted him with obvious delight, "Did you get the diary?"

Jackie could not help wishing that the excitement in the other's voice were for him and not for the prospect of getting back the diaries.

"Yes and no," he answered. "I lost my boys last night but I have a new lead. Unless I'm mistaken I'll have it this afternoon."

"Oh, how wonderful! I can't tell you how pleased I am to hear that. Will you be bringing them over here to the hotel?"

"I'll call first," Jackie told him. "Tell Dingo to stick around. One way or the other, I should have some news by three o'clock."

"He's out just now but I'll tell him," Steve promised.

With that out of the way, Jackie ordered breakfast and showered while he waited for the food to be delivered. His body still tingled with the memory of Bruce and the prospect of still another torrid session with the devilish blond. He could not help hoping that somehow he could free Bruce from the clutches of B.U.T.C.H. as well. No one who could be so divine sexually could be all bad, after all.

He moved his soapy hand away from the spot where it had lingered almost too long. It was just such thoughts that had awakened him this morning in an aroused state and his blood was still warm with eagerness.

His food was there by the time he stepped from the steaming shower. He wrapped a towel around his hips and ate wolfishly. Sex always increased his appetite and unless Bruce had cooled down quite a bit he would need a lot of energy later.

With breakfast out of the way, Jackie dressed and began packing his clothes. Barring any snags he might be ready to leave the hotel before the day was out. Then, with still some time to kill, he left the hotel and wandered about on the streets, an innocent looking tourist enjoying some of the sights of the city.

* * * * * * *

A little before two, he caught a cab and gave the address of Bruce's apartment. His excitement mounted with each passing block. If only Bruce hadn't failed or slipped up in any way.

Following Bruce's instructions, he circled around to the rear of the building and entered from that way. At Bruce's door, he saw the *Do Not Disturb* sign fastened to the door with a thumbtack. With a sigh of relief, he rapped lightly on the door.

Bruce greeted him with a pleased grin, motioning him quickly inside.

"Did you get it?" Jackie asked anxiously. As much as he was looking forward to seeing Bruce, the diary was still his first concern.

"I told you I can be cagey," Bruce reminded him. He opened a drawer of the desk and pulled out the notebook. Jackie recognized it at once as Dingo's diary. Luck was running with him again!

"Wonderful," he said enthusiastically. He threw his arms around the blond and hugged him happily.

"Now, do I get my reward?" Bruce asked with a flirtatious smile. "You promised me a repeat performance."

"That's a promise I'll be happy to keep," Jackie assured him. His lips sought and found the sweet full ones waiting for him. Bruce's tongue, a fiery sword, searched his mouth, darting about sensuously.

"I half expected to find you waiting for me naked again," Jackie whispered, his tongue tickling one pink ear.

"That can be quickly taken care of," Bruce assured him. Their bodies, crushed together in an embrace, were both rocklike with anticipation.

They walked together into the bedroom. Jackie was pleased by the way Bruce watched him as he undressed, his eyes gleaming more brightly as each article of clothing was shed.

There was no rush this time. They took it slowly, kissing one another tenderly, hands stroking healthy, young bodies. Jackie lay entranced as Bruce's flicking tongue examined all of him, starting smoldering fires in countless places. Bruce's hands tugged at him, turning him over and Jackie consented silently. Tit for tat, he reminded himself. The tongue explored his back, moving lower until his buttocks too were treated to delights. He felt the first, cautious attempt of Bruce to take him and raise up to meet the advance. There was a moment of pain that grew into an intense thrill as Bruce pushed against him. Bruce's fingers closed about Jackie's throbbing flesh, stroking slowly at first and then with increasing speed and fervor.

Their sweating bodies slapped together and rolled until Bruce was on his back and Jackie atop him. Jackie closed his eyes and flung his head back, his nostrils flaring. He twisted, seeking Bruce's mouth. There was no pain now, only the blinding heat of their furious loving. Beneath them the bed creaked and groaned with the frenzy of their movements.

Bruce was frantic, raging beyond control now. Jackie welcomed his thrusts, felt them grow more violent as the end neared. Their finish was a torrent that swept through them wildly, a shuddering, choking eternity of spasms that died away slowly, its sweetness lingering.

* * * * * * *

Afterward they showered together, playfully teasing one another. Their wrestling ended in an embrace and a long, happy kiss that resulted in renewed excitement. With the water of the shower pouring about him, Jackie stood with his legs braced apart. Bruce, kneeling before him, once again paid homage to his true master. When it was over, Jackie was beginning to ache with the exertion.

"Come on," he said, whacking the blonde's naked buttocks with a towel. "I need to catch my breath."

They lay happily in one another's arms across the bed. Music from a nearby radio drifted in through the open window.

"Haven't you ever thought about leaving the organization?" Jackie asked finally, making his bid for Bruce's future assistance. Now that the diaries were in his possession he was eager to deal with B.U.T.C.H. further. "Like going straight?"

Bruce seemed sad as he thought of the question. "Oh yes, I've thought about it. But it isn't possible, you know. B.U.T.C.H. doesn't allow anyone to resign."

Jackie knew what he meant. When one left the ranks of the outfit he was never able to tell anyone about the group.

"I could see that you're protected," Jackie assured him. "C.A.M.P. would look out for you, get you out of town if necessary. Besides, there wouldn't be any danger if we were able to break them up."

"No one can do that," Bruce argued. "They're too wily and too strong."

"C.A.M.P. could do it," Jackie insisted, determined to sway the young man. "If you'd only tell me how to find their headquarters."

Bruce studied him for a long minute. "If I did, would it mean that I could continue seeing you? On a serious basis?"

Jackie leaned over and planted a kiss in the vicinity of Bruce's thighs. "It's sweet of you to ask that," he said, meeting Bruce's eyes evenly. "But I couldn't promise you that, not even as badly as I want to get hold of those beasts. I'm not the sort to settle down, even with someone I like as much as you."

"But I could see you some times?" Bruce pursued his eyes wide and hopeful.

"I'm always in the mood for your sort of entertaining," Jackie told him.

Bruce was silent and thoughtful for a moment. "All right," he said finally in a nervous voice. "I'll do it, for you and for myself."

Jackie was beside himself with excitement. "You're great," he exclaimed, hugging him ecstatically.

100

Bruce's smile was pleased but still anxious, "I think I'd better have a drink," he said, getting up from he bed. "This is the most difficult decision I've ever made in my life."

"And the wisest," Jackie said somberly. "Make that two drinks."

He watched as Bruce crossed the room. The nude cheeks jiggled and bounced bewitchingly with each step and Jackie found his excitement returning, his body rising to action again.

The knife seemed to come from nowhere, appearing in the center of Bruce's wide back as though by magic. There was a second of frozen motion as Bruce stood rooted to the spot. Then, as Jackie jumped to his feet in horror, the blond crumpled and fell to the floor.

Jackie dived for his gun, throwing himself low. There was no one at the window now. With the gun in his hand he raced to it and stuck his head out in time to catch a glimpse of a familiar figure just jumping from the bottom of the old, iron fire escape. Jackie lifted the gun but there was no time to aim and fire before Fred had disappeared around the corner of the building.

With an oath Jackie turned and hurried back to the figure on the floor. The aim had been perfect. Bruce was already breathing his last.

His eyelids fluttered and he looked up into Jackie's face with glazed eyes. The ghost of a smile played over his lips.

"Don't talk," Jackie warned with a breaking voice, although he knew it was too late to do anything now. "I'll get a doctor."

"Fisherman's Wharf," Bruce managed to whisper. He tried to say something else but the sound he produced was only a sputtering gasp. His head rolled on Jackie's arm, his body jerked once and he was dead.

Jackie lowered the limp body to the floor and brushed away the tears that had clouded his eyes. B.U.T.C.H. was adding rapidly to the score he had to settle with them.

♠ CHAPTER TEN ♠
λ

Jackie dressed quickly, forcing aside the numbing sadness that threatened to engulf him. He had to think clearly now. There was no time for grief. Later he would be able to think about Bruce and cry for him, but now he had other things to occupy him: Dingo Stark and the diary which he had at least managed to repossess, and B.U.T.C.H. More than ever he was determined to put an end to that evil organization.

He left the apartment, taking the diary with him. On the street he was wary lest Fred still be around, waiting for an opportunity to seize the diary again. He saw no one and managed to flag a cab quickly. Once, looking out the back window of the taxi, he thought he recognized the car behind him as the same one he had followed from Golden Gate Park to Chinatown, but he was not certain and when he looked again it was not to be seen.

Back at his hotel he paused in the lobby and called the police from a pay phone, to inform them of Bruce's death, hanging up before there was time to trace a call. When he reached his room he placed a call at once to Dingo. Once again it was Steve who answered the phone.

"Did you get it," Steve asked anxiously.

"I got it," Jackie said grimly. And so, he thought silently, had Bruce.

"You sound angry," Steve said.

"I am," Jackie answered. "But I can't explain just now. Is Dingo there?"

"He's out again," Steve answered. "But he should be back shortly. Can you bring the diary over now?"

Jackie hesitated briefly. The safest place for the diary, he knew, would be with the local office of C.A.M.P. But Steve had a right to be concerned and want to see the book himself.

It was puzzling and even annoying that Dingo, who had so much at stake, did not seem concerned enough about the diary's recovery to be on hand for the call, but that, Jackie reminded himself, was his privilege.

"I'll bring it over," he said aloud into the phone.

"Oh, by the way," Steve said almost as an afterthought, "We've changed rooms."

Jackie repeated the new room number before hanging up. Then, still carrying the diary with him, he headed for the hotel in which Dingo and Steve were staying.

He was delayed briefly in the lobby of their hotel by a procession of lovely ladies in Eastern garb, their multi-colored saris brilliantly conspicuous. He remembered vaguely reading of the visit of a woman from India, a Princess of some importance

COLOR HIM GAY, BY VICTOR J. BANIS

in her country's political life. No doubt she was staying in the same hotel and this was her entourage. They were surrounded by a circle of guards who were at pains to see that the ladies were protected from reporters and curious bystanders.

The group took over the elevators, leaving the other guests to wait until they had been delivered to their floor.

Jackie made it at last to Steve's room. Steve answered his knock quickly, his dark eyes wider than ever with excitement. Jackie handed the diary over to him.

Steve stared at it for a moment and even thumbed through a page or two as though unable to believe his eyes. Finally he looked back at Jackie, beaming with happiness. Jackie's bad mood melted somewhat in the radiance of that smile and the muscles in the pit of his stomach began to tingle.

"Oh, Jackie, I can't tell you how happy you've made me," he said. He raised his arms and stepped forward. Jackie took him into an embrace willingly, his blood racing as the delicate body melted against his.

I shouldn't be doing this, he told himself silently, Dingo will hate me. But he *was* doing it and when he found the ruby lips near his own, waiting to be conquered, he could not prevent himself from burying them under his own mouth.

Far from protesting or withdrawing, Steve returned the kiss with the same ardent enthusiasm, his slender hands clinging to Jackie's shoulders. Whatever resistance Jackie might have had out of deference to Dingo was weakening rapidly.

They ended the kiss at last. Both of them, as their faces separated, were shaken by the emotion they had touched in one another.

"Dingo's still out." Steve whispered breathlessly. "We're alone here."

Jackie stared into the depths of the dark eyes. It was like plunging into a smoldering volcano. Steve might look fragile and delicate but beneath that milk white skin was a raging tempest of passion waiting to be set free.

"Is that a suggestion?" Jackie asked.

"I want to show you how grateful I am to you," Steve said in that throaty voice that sent shivers up and down Jackie's spine. "I know Dingo would want me to please you."

"Is that your only reason?" Jackie asked. Eager or not, he liked to think that he could arouse something more than gratitude in the lovely creature in his arms.

Steve laughed softly and shook his face. "I want you," he whispered, pressing his body tightly against the welcoming hardness of Jackie's. "I've wanted you since I first saw you."

It was the sort of answer that left no room for argument. Jackie kissed him again, all but bursting his seams with desire. His hands made their way down the graceful curve of Steve's back, grasping at the gently rounded orbs below.

"I want to see you," Steve hissed. "I want to see all of you, please."

"Always happy to oblige," Jackie said. At the moment he would have stood on his head if that was the way Steve wanted it.

He stepped back and began to undress, peeling off his clothes rapidly. He was impatient to be done with the preliminaries, aching with desire to explore Steve's maddening body.

Steve watched him with wide eyes, a faint smile playing upon his lips. The shirt went and then the T-shirt. Jackie kicked off his shoes, tugging at his socks. His trousers fell to the floor and he stood, finally clad only in his briefs, the fabric stretched ludicrously where Jackie's arousal was evident.

"The shorts too," Steve insisted. Jackie complied, rolling them down over his hips and bending to pull them down. He heard the scrape of a drawer opening as he stepped out of them and an ominous click. He raised his eyes and found himself staring down the barrel of a .45 automatic.

* * * * * * *

He groaned and started to pull his shorts back up.

"No, take them off," Steve snapped, waving the gun warningly.

"Don't tell me you're going to do anything with this now." Jackie said, indicating his conspicuous arousal. "Guns tend to cool my passion anyway."

"Take them off," Steve insisted. Jackie shrugged and did as ordered. There's nothing sillier, he thought glumly, then to stand naked in this condition and talk about anything but sex.

"Don't tell me you're working for B.U.T.C.H.?" he asked when he had kicked his shorts aside.

"Not at all," Steve assured him. "Although I did do some business with them. They came to me a while back to see if I could give them any dirt about Dingo. They were offering a generous price, so I told them about him and me."

It was logical of course, and a glaring fact that Jackie had overlooked altogether. B.U.T.C.H. could only have known about Dingo and Steve from one of two sources and obviously they hadn't gotten their information from Dingo.

"But why?" he asked aloud, bewildered. "He was your friend, more than that even. Why would you sell him out like that?"

Steve sneered, his pretty face turned vicious and unattractive. "My friend? Oh sure, he was crazy about me when we lived in those lousy tenements and I was the best lover he could get. Things were fine then. But what happened when he got his big breaks? It was good-bye to little Stevie then; he couldn't afford to be my friend. He's the big star and I get a trip to this country and a few dollars a month. Well, it wasn't enough, if you want to know the truth."

"Okay, so you got back at him," Jackie said. "You sold him out and made yourself some money. Why not leave it at that? Why give B.U.T.C.H. the diary as well?"

"Not B.U.T.C.H.," Steve corrected him. "I'm taking this for Dingo. He was willing to pay them if you hadn't gotten it back and he'll pay me too."

Jackie felt sick as he contemplated what a shock this would be for Dingo, betrayed by the one person he had most trusted.

"What about me?" Jackie asked. "Or don't you have any scruples about murder either?"

"Oh, I won't murder you," Steve said with wide-eyed innocence. "I just want to keep you out of the way until I get in touch with Dingo and make a deal. That's why I wanted your clothes off."

As he spoke he stopped and began gathering up Jackie's clothes, keeping the gun carefully trained on Jackie as he did so.

Jackie saw the logic. He could scarcely go out into the crowded hotel in downtown San Francisco in the raw, without getting himself arrested. And it would take him quite a while to convince the police of his story, long enough for Steve to put his plans in action.

Steve had crammed the clothes into an empty suitcase. He snapped it shut and set it by the door, putting the diary next to it. "Just to be sure you don't get yourself rescued," he said. He went to the telephone and, grabbing the wires, yanked them free of the wall. "I left your keys and your money," he said, indicating the small pile of things he had left on the floor. "So that things won't be too difficult for you later."

"You're forgetting one thing," Jackie told him, too angry to think of caution. "Dingo will be coming back here eventually."

"Not to this room," Steve said, unperturbed. "I forgot to tell you, when we changed rooms we took separate rooms, just to be cautious. And I left a message at the desk that they were not to disturb me in this room until morning. So you see, you'll be very much to yourself until the maid comes in the morning. I trust you'll be able to explain things to her."

He tucked the diary under his arms and picked up the suitcase. "It is a pity," he said, casting his eyes up and down Jackie's naked, although no longer excited, body. "You are lovely. I wasn't exaggerating when I said I wanted you. Maybe the next time...."

"Don't count on it." Jackie snapped. Steve only smiled and blew him a kiss as he slipped out the door.

Jackie seated himself morosely on the edge of the bed and contemplated his situation. It was dark outside, but the streets of San Francisco were too well lighted to allow him to wander about in the raw, even if he could get out of the hotel without being noticed. If Steve had left the phone intact he could have called someone to bring him clothes. As it was, he was in a state of isolation as surely as if the doors and windows had bars on them.

Without much hope he stood and went to the closet, peering inside. There was nothing left in the way of wearing apparel. He stood and surveyed the room, studying it sharply for any ideas.

His eyes fell upon the drapes, brightly colored and striped, and a glimmer of hope sprang into his mind as he remembered the entourage of women from India he had seen in the lobby. After all, he thought, a smile spreading across his face, Scarlet O'Hara had dressed herself in her draperies. Of course she had been able to sew them up a bit, but with a little effort he should be able to produce something similar to the saris he had seen earlier.

Working rapidly, he pulled the chair to the window and removed the drapes, spreading them out on the floor. At least there was plenty of material to work with. It was a wild gamble but it was his only hope of getting out of the hotel and back to his own room, where his other clothes waited for him.

He began draping the material around himself. Without pins or thread he would have to depend upon a few well tied knots and a lot of luck to keep the costume together. But, the Romans, he reminded himself, had used no fastenings in their togas. Of course, they had not had to face the crowds of San Francisco either.

He wrapped one panel about his body, under the armpits and continued wrapping until he had produced what appeared to be a cross between a sari and a mummy covering. The other panel he draped over his head, allowing it to fall about his shoulders as a combination headdress and blouse. Finally he tucked one end of the headpiece over the lower half of his face, leaving only his eyes and forehead exposed.

The result, as he studied it in the mirror, was far from setting fashion trends, but it was not so different from the costumes the women had worn through the lobby. He tucked his billfold and his keys into a loosely formed pocked in the folds of his skirt. It was now or never.

With a silent prayer for luck, he opened the door and stepped into the hall. It was empty and he walked hurriedly to the elevator.

Unfortunately, the elevator was occupied. Worse, Jackie recognized the tall, bird-like woman at once. Greta Romney was from his own city of

Los Angeles, a well known gossip columnist and notorious newshound. He knew at once, without question, that she was here in the city for one reason: to interview the visiting Princess from India. And he knew too that her nose for news would catch the scent of an interview with one of the Princess' traveling companions.

He half stepped back from the elevator but it was too late. Greta Romney's eyes had grown huge with surprise and delight as she saw him. With a feeling of despair, he stepped into the elevator.

"Oh, you're with the Princess' entourage aren't you?" Miss Romney asked quickly.

Jackie nodded his head; at least his costume was a success. If only he could feign ignorance of the language and somehow escape from Greta Romney before the situation grew any worse.

"I'm Greta Romney," she said rapidly. "And I've been trying so hard to get an interview with the Princess. If I could even talk with you for a few minutes...?"

Jackie's mind was racing. Perhaps he could ditch her by getting off on the floor where the Princess was staying. But which one had it been? Hopefully, he pushed a button and the elevator whooshed to a stop.

"Oh please, if you could only spare a minute or two. My suitcase is upstairs." Greta Romney followed him from the elevator, close at his shoulder.

In his eagerness to escape from the woman Jackie failed to notice the train that had come loose from his skirt and was trailing behind him. The doors of the elevator glided shut, catching the fabric. The material tore and the sudden jerk sent Jackie off balance and nearly caused him to fall.

"Damn," he exclaimed angrily under his breath.

The exclamation brought an expression of shock to Miss Romney's withered face, followed by one of glee. "Oh, you do speak the language?" she exclaimed happily.

Jackie groaned inwardly. Things were getting out of hand. Ahead of him a door opened and someone paused to finish a conversation in a foreign tongue. He had picked the right floor for the princess, but now he was in danger of being exposed as an imposter.

"Of course," he answered Miss Romney in a falsetto voice that he had used with success in the past when a case had necessitated his impersonating a woman. "And I'll be happy to grant you an interview."

If Miss Romney was surprised by the reversal, she was also quick to seize the opportunity. "How wonderful," she exclaimed, piloting him deftly back into the elevator. "It won't take but a minute."

As the doors of the elevator closed behind them Jackie had a glimpse of one of the Indian entourage staring after them in bewilderment.

Miss Romney's suite was on the top floor of the building. As they entered it, Jackie wondered briefly if he might be able to exchange his costume for one of Miss Romney's, but he quickly discarded the idea. He would hardly have an opportunity to make such a change and get away from Miss Romney without some alarms being raised by her. Even so, changing into a Western style costume would leave him in need of a wig and other items to conceal his masculinity.

"Can I offer you a drink?" Miss Romney asked when they were in the living room of the suite.

"Yes, thank you," Jackie answered in his falsetto.

"I'll order them sent up," Miss Romney said, going toward the phone. "They're very quick here."

"Sherry for me, please," Jackie said. As he spoke, he crossed the room quickly. Miss Romney's back was to him as she dialed the phone but she was nearer the door than he and he could hardly bolt down the hall with her in pursuit.

The second room of the suite was a bedroom but there was no door opening into the hall. Jackie glanced about wildly. The only other exit was the open window. He stuck his head out that and peered down. Fourteen stories below, the street was alive with evening traffic. He shuddered as he imagined falling that distance.

Only a few inches below the sill of the window, however, was a narrow ledge that encircled the building. It was not the safest looking means of escape but it was the only readily available route.

Miss Romney was still on the phone, her back to him. Jackie yanked his skirt up and hoisted himself quickly up and over the sill. Balancing himself precariously, he inched away from the window. As he made his way slowly and cautiously along the ledge he could hear Miss Romney behind him ordering drinks from room service.

114

His trembling hand touched the glass of another window and he examined it stealthily. It was open and the room inside was dark. Steeling himself for any encounter, Jackie raised himself to the sill and scramble over, dropping into the room. He landed, not on the floor as he had expected but across the width of an obviously occupied bed. Two figures jumped to sitting position.

A girl's voice gasped. The man croaked hoarsely, "My God, we're caught red handed. It's my wife."

"Excuse me," Jackie whispered in his feminine voice, trying to free himself from the tangle of limbs. "But I'm not your wife at all."

"You're not?" The voice was doubtful.

"No, I'm not, and I must say, I'm glad of it." He managed to get one foot to the floor and struggled to free his hand, which had somehow become pinned beneath a rather heavy posterior.

"Well then, what the hell are you doing pouncing upon us this way?"

"Poopsie, what's it all about?" the woman's voice whined.

"I didn't pounce upon you, I fell." The other foot reached the floor but his hand remained trapped. With a burst of inspiration, Jackie pinched at the weight upon it. The weight responded with a wriggle.

"Poopsie, stop that. Not until we find out what this is all about."

"It was such a lovely night, I decided to get some air," Jackie said sighing wearily. "And as soon as you give me my hand back, I'll be on my way."

With a shrill cry, the woman moved and Jackie found his hand free at last. He stood quickly, straining his eyes into the darkness. "Which way is out?"

"Would you like to use the door or would you prefer another window?" the man asked caustically.

"Never mind, I'll find it." Jackie shuffled into the blackness and collided with a wall. "Damn!"

His hand found the light switch. He flipped it on in exasperation, flooding the room with light.

"Good heavens, woman, have you no sense of decency?" the man demanded from the bed.

"Me?" Jackie asked, without looking back. He was already well acquainted with their state of dress—or undress, as it were. "At least I'm clothed."

The door was to his left and he opened it cautiously to peer out. The hall was empty, the stairwell only a few feet from him. At that moment he heard Miss Romney's voice from the neighboring room.

"Yoo hoo, Princess, are you hiding? It's only me, you needn't be afraid."

The voice grew louder as Miss Romney neared the hall. Jackie dashed madly for the stairs, leaving the door behind him ajar.

The man on the bed rose angrily, striding across the room to close the door. He had nearly reached the opening when a frenzied Miss Romney appeared in it.

"Excuse me," she gasped breathlessly, taking no apparent notice of his nudity. "Have you seen an Indian Princess?"

"Good God," he snorted, slamming the door violently in her face, "does this look like an embassy?"

THE MAN FROM C.A.M.P.

♠ CHAPTER ELEVEN ♠
λ

On the next floor down, Jackie took a chance on the elevator again. This time it was empty and he rode to the lobby,

Although he attracted considerable attention as he passed through the lobby, no one attempted to bother him or stop him. He reached the sidewalk outside and half walked, half ran to the nearest taxicab parked there.

"The Essex," he snapped in his natural voice as he jumped inside. The cab driver gave him a startled look, but he shrugged philosophically and climbed behind the wheel. He asked no questions on the way and Jackie rewarded his silence with a generous tip.

The entrance into his own hotel was even more of an ordeal since there was more danger here that he might be recognized. To his dismay the elevator operator was his knowing friend. Jackie reverted to his falsetto and, although the operator gave him a few sidelong glances, he did not apparently recognize the figure behind the drapery veil. With a big sigh of relief Jackie reached his room at last.

He shed the costume and without taking time to dress again called Dingo at his hotel. Things were getting out of hand rapidly. He would have to warn Dingo of Steve's betrayal but that was not the sort of thing he wanted to explain on the phone. For the moment his immediate concern was getting Dingo safely out of the way.

To his relief Dingo was in his room. Steve apparently had not yet approached him about the diary. Probably he had been preparing things so that he could disappear conveniently afterward.

"Jackie," Dingo greeted him anxiously. "What's the news?"

"Plenty," Jackie answered. "But I can't explain on the phone. I want you to leave your hotel, right now, and come over here."

"I'll have to wait for Steve," Dingo said innocently. "He's out just now, but he shouldn't be too long."

"I'll take care of Steve," Jackie assured him with sincerity. He had every intention of taking care of Steve, although not in the sense that Dingo would interpret the remark. "Just get over here fast."

"If you say so," Dingo agreed. "I'll be there in twenty minutes."

With that taken care of, Jackie dressed, again tucking the Derringer into its holster. Once Dingo was safely here he had quite a few chores to be attended to. There was the matter of finding Steve and retrieving the diary. After that there was Fisherman's Wharf, the place that Bruce had mentioned as he was dying. Unless he was sadly mistaken, Bruce

120

had been trying to tell him something about the headquarters of B.U.T.C.H.

* * * * * * *

Twenty minutes later Dingo was still not there. Jackie gave him five more minutes and then called the hotel again. There was no answer at Dingo's room. Cursing himself, Jackie started off for Dingo's hotel, watching the street for any sign of the singer.

"Any idea where I might find Mr. Benton?" he asked at the desk, using the name under which Dingo had registered at the hotel. "It's important that I reach him."

"He went out a little while ago," the man at the counter explained. "I'm sure he'll be returning however, if you'd care to try later."

"Did he leave any messages?" Jackie asked impulsively.

"Only for a Mr. Holmes," the clerk informed him.

Jackie felt a sinking sensation in his stomach. "I'm Mr. Holmes," he said quickly. "What was the message?"

The clerk's eyes were wide with surprise. "But you can't be. Mr. Holmes was here just a few minutes ago."

Jackie stared at him in shock and fear. "I mean," the clerk went on, frightened by the way Jackie was looking at him. "A gentleman who said he was Mr. Holmes was here. I gave him the message."

"What did it say?" Jackie demanded.

"Oh dear, I don't know. But he didn't take it with him, I don't think. Wait...." the flustered clerk stooped down and rummaged through a wastebasket. "Yes, here it is," he said, producing a crumpled slip of paper.

Jackie read the message in one glance: "Have gone to meet Steve at Union Square. He said it was urgent and not to call you. Will check with you later."

So Steve was already springing his trap. And, far worse, someone else knew about it, someone who had used his name to claim this message. That someone could only be from B.U.T.C.H.

"I hope I didn't do anything wrong," the clerk was saying in an agitated voice. "I thought..."

"Don't worry about it," Jackie told him, starting for the door.

Those diaries were dangerous. B.U.T.C.H. might go to any lengths to get them back from Steve. The situation at Union Square could be an explosive one. He ignored the motions of the cab drivers in front of the hotel and began to run down the sidewalk. The park was only a few blocks away. He could be there faster on foot than in a car in the evening traffic.

Union Square occupied one small city block in the heart of the city. Beneath the neat lawns of the park was a multilevel parking garage. He had no way of knowing whether Steve and Dingo would be in the park itself or below in the garage, but wherever they were he had to find them, and fast.

The passersby stared after him as he ran with the speed of a gazelle. Fortunately, as a runner his times equaled nearly every world record. Still, even in San Francisco the sight of a neatly dressed young man racing as though for his life was peculiar. It was not his own life, however, that he was racing for.

He saw them when he was still almost a block away. As luck would have it they were in plain sight, near the end of one of the walks that cut diagonally across the park. Even at the distance he could see that they were arguing and that Dingo was furiously angry. Steve, then, had made his demands and Dingo, hurt by the betrayal, had lost his fiery temper. There was always the possibility that Steve might relent. After all, he had once been fond of Dingo. But there was also the possibility that Steve might lose his temper as well and do something really rash—and he was carrying a .45 automatic.

The trouble, however, did not come from Steve. Even as Jackie was racing toward the intersection of the street that separated them from him, he saw a familiar car reach the corner and slow down. He recognized the driver at once as Bruno Scotto. His two thugs, with him as always, jumped from the car and headed for Dingo and Steve.

Ignoring the traffic light that was against him, Jackie dashed across the street, dodging cars wildly.

The move was a bold one, dependent upon speed and surprise. Only a very few of the people around were aware of what was happening. Dingo was struck and fell to the sidewalk holding his head. The two men grabbed Steve and dragged him toward the open car door.

Jackie caught one of them in a flying tackle that sent both of them rolling across the cement. The man was fast to recover and skilled as a fighter. He broke free of Jackie's grip and started for his partner who was struggling to get Steve in the car.

"Jackie," Steve yelled. "The diary!" As he yelled he managed to free one arm and threw the briefcase that he was carrying onto the sidewalk.

Instinctively Jackie dived for it. He got it, but he had given the trio of thugs the seconds necessary to make their escape, taking Steve with them. Even as Jackie headed for them again, the car pulled away into the steam of traffic.

Dingo was on his feet and came toward him. A small crowd of spectators had begun to form about them. Jackie opened the briefcase and saw the diary inside.

"Take this," he told Dingo. "And hightail it back to my hotel. Go to the elevator operator, a homely young man, and tell him you're another of my brothers. He'll understand and see that you get into my room. Don't leave there under any circumstances."

"But where will you be?" Dingo asked. "And what about Steve? He tried to blackmail me too but I don't want to see him killed."

"I'll try to prevent it." Jackie said. He took a notepad from the pocket of his jacket and scribbled a number on it. "Here," he said, thrusting the paper into Dingo's hand. "This is my local contact here. Call him from the hotel. Tell him you're calling for me and that I've gone to Fisherman's Wharf."

He didn't wait for further argument, nor was it necessary. As he headed for the curb and an approaching cab, Jackie glanced back and saw Dingo, still looking puzzled but starting obediently in the direction of the hotel.

"Fisherman's Wharf," Jackie said as he jumped into the cab. He sat impatiently on the front edge of the seat, wishing he had been able to follow Bruno and his henchmen. He had no way of knowing whether they were headed to Fisherman's Wharf also or some other location. And there was no telling what they might do to Steve out of pure anger. Steve had tried to betray them and they had killed Bruce for the same thing.

* * * * * * *

Fisherman's Wharf in San Francisco was an experience unto itself. Restaurants and shops lined the water's edge, and the water was crowded with boats of every description: small fishing crafts, sightseeing boats, even an old sailing ship that had been turned into a sort of floating museum. Further out in the bay was the dim outline of Alcatraz Island, once a name to instill fear in the hearts of lawbreakers, now only of interest to the tourists.

Along the walks, open stalls offered servings of fresh shrimp and crabs and chowder. The intoxicating aromas filled the air, blending with the ever-present scent of the sea.

Moving along with the evening crowds of sightseers, Jackie was only half aware of the colorful atmosphere about him. His senses were attuned to the scene about him but it was not enjoyment or pleasure that he sought. Somewhere within this relatively small area was the clue for which he was searching, the reason Bruce had sent him here.

He found his clue at last and rather unexpectedly. At one point along the walk a barker was extolling the pleasure of a boat cruise of the harbor. His success was something less than inspiring, due to the lateness of the hour and the chill of the evening air. One of the two launches was just returning with its handful of passengers, while the other was preparing to depart with only four people aboard.

As Jackie neared the gate where the tickets were purchased for the trip he glanced in the direction of the launch that was now landing and his heart skipped a beat. It was none other than Fred, Bruce's assailant, piloting the boat. Quickly Jackie approached the gate and purchased a ticket.

"That's it for tonight," the manager was shouting to Fred. "May as well call it a night."

"Fine with me," Fred called back. He left the boat and headed out through the gate. Jackie paused, looking away as Fred passed so close by him that they nearly touched. Perhaps he had made a wrong move. Fred might even now be preparing to leave the area by car.

As he paused, however, he saw Fred had merely approached one of the food stalls to purchase a late evening snack. Glancing about to be sure that he wasn't being noticed, Jackie decided to gamble. He darted lightly to Fred's boat and, before anyone could see him, he was aboard. A sheet of canvas had been tossed beside the sheltered cabin. Without hesitation he scrambled under it and waited. He did not have long to wait. A minute later the boat bobbed in the water as Fred climbed aboard.

The engine came to life again and the boat began to move slowly, pulling away from the Wharf. Huddled under the canvas, Jackie felt a

126

surge of confidence. Soon they had passed Alcatraz and were moving along at a fast speed.

The engines began to slow. Jackie ventured another look. At first the area around him and the presence of other craft was puzzling. He realized then that they were across the bay, nearing the quaint town of Sausalito, a colorful village that was charmingly European, a haven for tourists and yachtsmen alike.

They were approaching another craft now, a massive, handsome yacht that floated silent and dark in the water. As Jackie watched from under the canvas, Fred cut the engines and drifted alongside the yacht.

There were a few minutes of muffled voices and furtive activity and then silence returned. Jackie guessed that Fred had boarded the yacht. "Should I do likewise?" he asked himself. This could be an important meeting with others from the group or it could be an insignificant visit with friends. If he remained here he would never know what was on board the other craft. But if he boarded the yacht he would be sure to lose Fred when he left.

He reached his decision. Slipping from beneath the canvas, he crept stealthily along the wet dock. There was only silence above him. If a guard were posted he would be walking right into a hornet's nest. He removed his Derringer from the holster and tensed for action, boarding the yacht.

There was no one in sight but now that he was closer he could hear the faint sound of low-pitched voices. They were in the cabin, talking rapidly but quietly. A dim light gleamed through one of the portholes. Crouching low, Jackie moved slowly toward it. He caught a glimpse of someone silhouetted against the sky: the guard, standing near the entrance to the cabin. Jackie froze, waiting until the man had moved slightly away, circling about the cabin. Then Jackie moved forward again.

He reached the porthole. Raising his head slowly, he peered inside. Fred was talking to someone with many gestures. His listener had his back to the opening so that Jackie saw nothing of him but leather-clad shoulders. Bruno Scotto was there too and his two sidekicks. And, Jackie saw with relief, so was Steve. Bound and gagged, he lay huddled on the floor of the cabin, his dark eyes bigger than ever with fright.

There was a call from behind him and for the first time Jackie was aware of the approach of another launch. Crouched where he was, he was trapped between the newcomer and the cabin. His eyes swept the deck for some place to hide and saw nothing.

Behind him the guard had gone out to greet the newcomer and was helping him aboard. Jackie risked another glance inside the cabin. This time though, he was spotted. Ironically it was not Fred, but Steve, who saw him first. Steve blinked and his body jerked with surprise. Fred saw the reaction and turned toward the window in time to see Jackie's face before he ducked.

There was a shout from inside the cabin and, at almost the same time, one from behind him. He had been spotted all right; and surrounded. A gunshot cracked from the direction of the guard and the wood over his head splintered with the impact of the bullet.

Jackie hit the deck. He had only one shot in the Derringer and there were at least seven of them, maybe more. Another shot tore the air over his head. The guard was getting too close, Jackie decided, and in the other direction the cabin door had been yanked open. He could not stay where he was. Raising himself on one knee, he fired his gun. There was a cry of pain and the guard toppled over.

The man with him jumped for the gun that had fallen to the deck. Jackie threw his Derringer. The weapon hit smartly across the man's head, stunning him momentarily.

Jackie dived for the gun as well but he other man reached it first. They grappled for an instant; then, suddenly, they were caught in the beam of a powerful light.

"Better hold it, Mr. Holmes," someone said from nearby. "Or I'll shoot to kill."

THE MAN FROM C.A.M.P.

♠ CHAPTER TWELVE ♠
λ

There was little that Jackie could do for the moment. Giving up the struggle for the gun, he stood, hands over his head.

"That's better, thank you," the speaker said. "I think perhaps you'd better come this way, to the cabin."

Jackie did as told, the entire pack of them circling about him, guns ready. Jackie gave Steve an apologetic look as they entered the cabin. He had hoped to save Steve, traitor or not, and perhaps give him a new start on life.

He turned finally to face his enemy and could not suppress an expression of astonishment. "Tiger Bey," he said softly.

Tiger Bey acknowledged his surprise with a smile. "In person," he said with a mock curtsey. "Now suppose you tell me about yourself."

"I'm Dorothy from Kansas," Jackie recited in a sing-song voice. "And I'm on my way to Oz."

"Very funny," Tiger snapped. "Perhaps it will save you any ideas if I tell you that I've already figured you out. When Fred reported your conversation with Bruce I did some checking. Unless I'm mistaken, you're the highly respected Jackie Holmes, agent for C.A.M.P."

"At your service," Jackie told him. There was no point in denying the fact. B.U.T.C.H.'s files on him would be extensive and accurate.

"Well, you've looked for me a long time," Tiger said. "Since you're going to die, I may as well give you a bit of satisfaction. This, my dear friend, is the headquarters you've been seeking for so long."

"This yacht?" Jackie said, surprised. "Then you...?"

"I am the head officer of B.U.T.C.H.," Tiger informed him smugly.

The yacht was local, Jackie thought quickly. No wonder they had had such a difficult time figuring out whether B.U.T.C.H. worked from Los Angeles or San Francisco. With a moving office they could work out of any watery area.

As for Tiger Bey, that too was a link he should have suspected. Although this was their first meeting, he had known of the man for years. With his brutishly male appearance, the Levi's and leather jacket, along with boots and other motorcycle gear, Tiger Bey was known not only to him but to police throughout the State. He was an impressive figure, the sort that inspired both fear and desire in the hearts of homosexuals.

He was also known to be the leader of a rat-pack motorcycle gang that often terrorized the small towns up and down the state. It was suspected as well that he was involved in numerous forms of vice, dope and prostitution among them. Jackie had never suspected, however, that the notorious figure was also the ringleader of B.U.T.C.H.

"Well, this is a night of surprises isn't it?" Jackie said aloud. "I can hardly wait to see what happens next."

"Next," Tiger informed him. "You and your insipid friend there will be killed."

"Why him?" Jackie argued. "He can't do you any harm. Why not send him on his way?"

"He tried to play games with us," Tiger snapped coldly. "No one fools around with us and lives to tell about it."

Someone appeared at the door of the cabin to announce that everything was ready for departure.

"Tell them to get started," Tiger said. He turned back to the room. "Tie him up," he ordered, indicating Jackie.

The others were quick to do his bidding. Jackie's hands were bound in front of him and his feet tied as well, so that he could only sit helplessly on one of the upholstered benches attached to the walls.

The yacht had begun to move. "Isn't this a peculiar time for a cruise?" Jackie taunted his enemy. All the while his mind was racing madly, seeking some way out of the predicament.

"Strictly business," Tiger explained. "In the first place we can't just toss you in the water here. You would float ashore in no time. Besides we have an appointment about two miles out."

"An appointment?"

Tiger smiled evilly. "With a Japanese freighter that's headed for San Francisco. Included in its cargo, although not in the import declarations, is a sizable amount of opium. We'll have to unload that before it reaches the harbor."

Opium, Jackie thought with dismay, to be loaded into this yacht and then unloaded at some carefully chosen point along the coast. Was there no crime so foul that these people would not turn it to a profit?

"We'll take care of you two after we get that loaded," Tiger was saying. "I don't think I need worry about you. Even if you get free, and I understand you're quite clever, the Bay is a dangerous place for a swim. In a few minutes we'll be well on our way, and besides, there are sharks in these waters, as you well know."

"And then back to San Francisco?" Jackie encouraged him to talk. While he was still alive there was always the possibility of escape and this was a golden opportunity to gain as much information as possible.

"Oh no, it was getting a bit warm there. We'll start up anew somewhere else. That's what we were waiting for, you see. Our files, photographs and such had to be loaded on board. Our headquarters are complete on this craft. We can start our business anywhere."

He turned from Jackie, terminating the conversation. "The men have been arguing about the other prisoner," he said to Fred, standing nearby. "Tell them to help themselves to him."

"What about him?" Fred asked, nodding his head in Jackie's direction.

"He's an honored guest," Tiger said with a grin. "I hardly think it would be fair to allow mere workmen to enjoy themselves with him. As a matter of fact, I may do him the honor of some physical pleasures myself; just before we kill him."

Tiger left the cabin. Bruno and his friends returned, grinning with pleasure as Fred told them they had permission to amuse themselves with Steve.

"You pigs," Jackie snapped angrily as the men began tearing Steve's clothes from him. For an answer, Bruno slapped him viciously across the face.

"Keep your mouth shut," the apelike man warned him. "Or I won't wait for permission to work you over."

"Come on," one of the others insisted. Steve's face was a study in terror. His clothes were in shreds, the delicate beauty of his nakedness exposed to the lustful eyes of his attackers. As Jackie watched helplessly they pinned the young man down to the floor.

Bruno was first. Jackie shuddered as the man pulled down his trousers, revealing the weapon with which he intended to claim the helpless body. It was terrifying, something for torture rather than pleasure.

Steve's cry of agony was audible even through the cloth that covered his mouth. He struggled helplessly in the hands of the men holding him, to no avail.

The assault was more vicious than anything Jackie had ever witnessed. Again and again, Bruno worked at the fragile body with long, crashing blows, his face contorted in savage pleasure. Mercifully, Steve fainted as the end neared.

"Wake him up," Bruno snarled when he had finished and risen from the floor. They slapped Steve's face until his eyes, glazed and unbelieving, opened again.

Each of them took turns. Their bodies and the floor were streaking with blood. Steve's smooth skin was a mass of bruises and cuts.

At last they could not rouse him again. The last of them took his turn anyway. When he had finished they kicked the limp body aside.

"Tie him up again," Bruno ordered. "In case he comes to."

With a horrible grin he advanced toward Jackie. "That get you excited?" he asked, chucking a finger under Jackie's chin. "Sure you don't want to join the party? I'm all raring to go again."

Jackie recognized the lust in Bruno's eyes and knew that the man was not merely talking. But he was sure that he would not easily disobey Tiger's orders. Tiger had marked him for his own and he would not want damaged goods.

"You filthy beast," Jackie told him coldly and unafraid. "Try untying my hands and see if you can manage me as easily."

Bruno only laughed. "Let's go," Fred said from the doorway. "We've got work to do. The fun's over for now."

They left, closing the door after themselves and extinguishing the light. In the darkness Jackie breathed a partial sigh of relief. He had not dared to attempt anything before. Now, with them gone, he could go to work again.

He pulled his bound hands down to the buckle of the belt he wore in his trousers. Carefully he guided the ropes to the bottom edge of the buckle, an edge ground to razor sharpness. One slip and he would slice his wrists open. Slowly, patiently, he began to cut the ropes.

It took several minutes to cut through the ropes but he dared not risk haste. Finally the ropes gave. He tugged hard at them and his hands were free. Working swiftly now, he untied his feet. At last he was able to stand again.

He worked in the dark, not wanting to risk the light. His first thought was for Steve and he hurriedly released him as well, carrying the limp body to a bench.

"Steve," he whispered, patting the swollen face gently. "It's Jackie."

Steve's eyelids fluttered at last. He opened them, first in terror. Then, as he recognized Jackie's face close above his own, he began to sob.

"Oh Jackie," he gasped. "I prayed I would die. I didn't think I could endure it any longer."

"It's okay," Jackie told him, keeping his voice low. "I'm trying to get us out of this. Can you manage to run or swim if we have to?"

"I don't know," Steve answered. He struggled to control his sobs bravely. "But I'll try."

With Jackie's help he managed to get to his feet but his legs were too weak to support him. He sat back down wearily.

"It's no use," he said hopelessly.

"Don't give up," Jackie said. He went to the porthole and peered out. The shore was already distant. Even if they could get off the boat there wasn't the slightest chance they could swim that far, not with Steve so weak.

There was something else to be considered, however. This yacht was the headquarters for B.U.T.C.H. and loaded aboard it were all of their files, the information with which they were able to ruin countless lives. If he could destroy it all, it would be worth his own life and Steve's.

* * * * * * *

They had not, fortunately, stripped him, mistakenly confident as they had been that the ropes would hold him. Stooping down, he hastily removed one shoe. As Steve watched him, puzzled, he twisted the heel aside to reveal a hidden compartment, containing a maze of batteries and wires.

"What is that?" Steve asked.

"A radio," Jackie explained, flicking the button that turned the transmitter on. "It sends out a signal that is automatically picked up at C.A.M.P. offices anywhere. But it's only a slim hope. It hasn't the power to transmit more than a mile or so. There's not much chance anyone in San Francisco will receive the S.O.S."

He kicked off the other shoe for convenience. Then, standing, he hurriedly peeled off his shirt and T-shirt. He lifted one arm over his head and with the other hand, yanked at the tuft of hair.

"Good heavens," Steve said, as the artificial skin came away to reveal Jackie's closely shaven armpit beneath. Without comment Jackie removed the plastic skin from the other side as well.

He tore the shallow layers of artificial skin apart, removing the small capsule hidden in each. Alone, the ingredients of the capsules were harmless. Combined, they created a powerful chemical explosion that could be detonated merely by impact. He mixed the ingredients with cautious hands and gently returned the mixture to the two capsules.

As he had suspected, the door was locked. He went back for the other shoe. Hidden in the heel of that one was a thin, deadly knife. Stooping before the door, Jackie inserted the blade into the lock. In a few seconds he heard a successful click, and the door was open.

Seconds were precious now. Each one carried them farther from the shore, already in the distance, and nearer the Japanese freighter they were meeting. He put an arm about Steve and helped him to his feet.

"We'll have to make a run for it," he said in a whisper. "If we can get to the side and over we might have a chance of getting away." He did not add that the chance was a slim one. If his plan worked, the radio in his shoe would be sunk along with the ship. Even so, it would take some time for anyone who might have received the signal to get to them.

They climbed the steps that led to the deck and paused. Only a few feet separated them from the rail and the icy water beyond. In one hand Jackie held the two highly explosive capsules. Would they be enough, he wondered, even as powerful as they were?

On the deck one of the guards was standing only a few feet from them, his back to them. Jackie would have to all but drag Steve across the deck. How long would it take the man to draw his gun and shoot: a few seconds? It would have to be long enough.

"Now," he hissed in Steve's ear. They rose and started forward, Steve barely able to hobble along. Behind them the guard whirled about, startled.

"Hit the deck," Jackie said, shoving Steve down as shots rang out. He raised his hand and hurled the first of the capsules back into the open door of the cabin. The explosion rocked the entire vessel and knocked the guard off his feet. Flames erupted from the interior of the cabin.

"Let's go," Jackie said. Steve however, remained limp. Jackie turned him over and saw the bullet hole in the center of his forehead. Steve wasn't going anywhere.

There was bedlam all around. People were shouting and the powerful light that had been turned on was sweeping the deck. It swept over Jackie and more shots rang out.

It was now or never. Jackie jumped to his feet. He hurled his second capsule toward the stern and the powerful engines. There was another massive explosion and a burst of flames.

Jackie dived for the rail, plunging downward. The icy water was like an electric shock. He swam furiously in long hard strokes. When his lungs felt as though they were bursting, he surfaced.

No one was worrying about him. The entire yacht seemed to be in flames. Even as Jackie paused to look back, the flames reached the fuel storage tanks. There were two more awful explosions that sent flames and wood high into the air.

The headquarters of B.U.T.C.H. was done for. But unless some miracle happened, so was he. The water was like ice, already numbing his limbs. He struck out in the direction of the shore, every muscle straining. His arms lifted and fell, his feet kicking powerfully. He was a championship swimmer and held records in numerous events, but this was a challenge beyond anything he had ever faced before.

* * * * * * *

His first thought, when the light fell across him, was that someone from the yacht was in pursuit. That, he realized, was impossible. He stopped, treading water as the powerboat roared toward him.

"My dear, what a time for a swim," a voice called out and Jackie recognized the gray-haired agent from C.A.M.P.

A minute later he was being helped aboard the boat and a blanket was wrapped around his shivering body. "How on Earth did you get here so fast?" he asked, clutching the blanket close.

"Your English friend called and sent us to Fisherman's Wharf," the agent explained. "Love, I've been combing this Bay with a tortoise shell comb ever since. I was about to head back for a good-morning cap when I got the S.O.S. of yours and here I am. The coast guard, by the by, is not far behind."

"Good, I've got some work for them," Jackie said. "That bonfire you see in the distance is what's left of B.U.T.C.H."

"Heavens," the agent exclaimed, peering at he burning yacht in the distance. "And me without a marshmallow."

* * * * * *

It was several hours later before everything had been cleaned up. The Coast Guard, alerted to the presence of the Japanese freighter, had made a successful haul there. As for B.U.T.C.H., one or two survivors had been rescued from the icy water and placed under arrest, although no trace had been found of Tiger Bey.

Finally, a weary Jackie was dropped off at his hotel. He ignored the stares produced by his bare feet and lack of shirt. It was not, after all, the most peculiar outfit he had worn on this case.

It was not until he opened the door of his room and saw the sleeping figure in his bed, back turned toward him, that he remembered Dingo. The singer was sound asleep, unaware of him.

Jackie suddenly felt less exhausted. Dingo, he saw, was accustomed to sleeping in the raw. He had kicked the covers aside and the view turned toward Jackie was an enticing one, the broad hips curved provocatively, the ripe buttocks sending a silent invitation.

With a smile, Jackie removed his trousers, leaving them in a heap on the floor. He lowered himself to the bed, sliding across its surface to press his own body against Dingo's warmth.

Dingo started. "Jackie?" he asked drowsily.

"Umm-hmm." Jackie said. His arm went around Dingo and down, seeking the remembered treasure.

"What are you doing?" Dingo asked. The muscles of his backside tensed as he felt the urgent firmness pressed against them.

"Collecting my reward," Jackie informed him. "For returning the diary."

"Oh," was all Dingo said. And then, a minute later, "Ouch. That hurts, blast it."

"Relax," Jackie whispered. His hand, in front, was busily helping Dingo to ignore the pain and Dingo was responding quickly.

Jackie was gentle and careful, advancing slowly, giving Dingo time to accustom himself to the innovation.

"How am I doing?" he asked, nibbling Dingo's ear.

Dingo snorted and wriggled his hips, sending a thrill of excitement through Jackie's body. "It might be fun," he said, "if you weren't being so bloody careful."

Jackie didn't need any further encouragement. He stopped being careful. For a brief second his thoughts strayed to his apartment in Los Angeles and particularly to his trophy, the huge carved phallus with its notches to signify his conquests. He reminded himself that he could carve a new notch on it when he got back.

His thoughts, however, did not remain long on that subject. Joyfully, they returned to the present—to the body in his arms and the pleasure of the moment.

♠ ABOUT THE AUTHOR ♠
λ

Lecturer, former writing instructor and early rab-ble-rouser for gay rights and freedom of the press, **VICTOR J. BANIS** *is the critically acclaimed author ("...a master storyteller"—*Publishers Weekly*) of more than 140 published novels and nonfiction works, and his verse and short pieces have ap-peared in numerous journals (*Blithe House Quar-terly, *Fall 2006) and anthologies (*Charmed Lives, *Lethe Press, 2006).*